THIRTEEN DAYS IN MILAN

"I'm Italian and I must say that Erickson's view of my country and my fellow citizens is not so stereotypical as it appears in other books about Italy written by a foreign writer. His understanding of our political and cultural situation is very deep, his knowledge about food and drinks amazing, and the characters in the story is powerful and realistic."

"The historical introduction to Italian politics is very interesting and give a great foundation for the rest of the book. Once you get to know the characters and the story is headed for a big climax it's hard to stop reading. While reading it was easy to visualize the scenes because of the attention to detail in descriptions of the environments, sounds and smells. If you enjoy John le Carre or Raymond Chandler you might enjoy this book."

NO ONE SLEEPS

". . . a chilling story that reads like today's headlines. With no leads, DIGOS agents use technology to discover the terrorists are using stolen phones to communicate. But the agents don't know that the Muslim's terrorist leader, an Italian with Pakistani heritage, was trained at a Taliban terrorist camp in Afghanistan."

"A thoroughly researched and soberly told tale of one of today's most pressing issues." — KIRKUS REVIEWS

"No One Sleeps is both entertaining and all too real. It is obvious that the author did a great deal of research and although it is fiction, many details are quite accurate, including the training camp in Pakistan. The book is action packed and would make a great movie. It has good plot and character development. I could not put it down."

D1572501

"Vesuvius Nights has everything I want in a mystery. A compelling plot, vivid writing, and an Italian setting with vivid details. Erickson's writing style really holds my attention and fully engages me. The pace of the writing mirrors the speed of modern life with the action transpiring over one week. The characters exhibit depth and humanity and become very real. Highly recommended."

"This third book in Jack Erickson's thriller series moves to Naples with the back story of the leading female detective, exploring the workings of the Camorra, organized crime. Jack's descriptions of Naples and the views of Vesuvius make you feel a part of the vibrant city, and the action will have you transfixed. Can't wait for the next one!"

VESUVIUS NIGHTS

JACK ERICKSON

RedBrick Press
www.jackerickson.com

ISBN: 978-0-941397-17-9

Printed in the United States of America

Cover and interior design by: 1106 Design

To Grace, William, Preston, Lukas, Campbell and Desirée
And, of course, to Marilyn

VESUVIUS NIGHTS

Camorra is a nonexistent word, a term of contempt used by narcs and judges, journalists and scriptwriters; it's a generic indication, a scholarly term relegated to history—a name that makes Camorristi smile. The word clan members use is System, "I belong to the Secondigliano System," an eloquent term, a mechanism rather than a structure. The criminal organization coincides directly with the economy, and the dialectic of commerce is the framework of the clans.

—Roberto Saviano
Gomorrah

CHAPTER ONE

MONDAY, MAY 4, 2015

On Wednesday, Antonella Amoruso would buy a casket in Napoli. She never expected she would face such a grisly task, but life has ways of putting emotional traumas in our paths. Death. Funeral. Burial. The end of a life.

No one likes to be reminded of their mortality. Funerals are grim reminders that death is a part of life and that, one day, friends and family will attend ours. Antonella hated funerals. She had attended three already this year. And it was only May.

The previous Saturday, she'd attended a funeral for an old friend, Cristina, killed in a car crash on the Autostrada A24. Antonella had bumped into Cristina at a café a week before the accident, and they agreed to have dinner that Saturday. Antonella made a reservation at a restaurant and left a voicemail with the time and place. But on Saturday, Antonella went to Cristina's funeral, not the restaurant.

In February, she went to the funeral for Arturo, her mentor at Milano's Questura, who had retired and was living on a farm in Piemonte with his wife of fifty-five years. Arturo was a gentleman, intelligent and patient, the kind of person you turned to in times of doubt or loneliness. She would have called Arturo when she got the news about Napoli, but of course, she couldn't. He was dead.

The third funeral had been for Bianca, a sixteen-year-old who had died of bulimia. She was the daughter of another friend. Bianca's classmates and friends filled the pews at the church, weeping, hugging each other, and sobbing when the casket was wheeled out of the church. Bianca's mother told Antonella that her daughter had been obsessed with losing weight, secretly taking laxatives and vomiting after meals.

The last thing Antonella had expected was to attend another funeral. Instead, she'd been focusing on her job as a senior deputy of Milano's Questura. They were now three days into a special event. From May through October, Milano would be on the world stage at the Expo, an international event held every five years in major cities around the world. Expo 2010 had been held in Shanghai; Dubai would be the host city in 2020.

Expo Milano 2015 was a once-in-a-lifetime event for Italia to showcase two thousand years of history and culture that had produced the Renaissance: the genius of Dante, Petrarch, Michelangelo, and Leonardo da Vinci; the cuisines of Napoli, Toscana, Sicilia, Milano, and Roma; the natural beauty of the Cinque Terre, Puglia, Amalfi, and the Alpine lakes—Como, Maggiore, Orta, and Garda.

The opening of Expo on Friday, the first of May, had been marred by riots on the streets of Milano, burning cars, anti-Expo left-wing protestors, and anti-globalist and environmentalist demonstrators in the streets, tossing petrol bombs and tear gas at police in full riot gear. Antonella was on a panel the following Monday morning with senior Carabinieri, Polizia di Stato, and Guardia di Finanza officers receiving briefings on the demonstrations and reviewing media coverage of the rioting that erupted after the official opening of the Expo by Italian Prime Minister Matteo Renzi at the Expo pavilion.

Antonella learned that she would be going to Napoli that week while she was attending a high-level police briefing at the Expo Milano 2015 pavilion north of town.

She read a text from her assistant, Monica, when the panel took a fifteen-minute break and immediately called her. "When did she call?" Antonella asked, weaving through the crowd of uniformed and plain-clothes police officials moving toward a buffet table for coffee, brioche, biscotti, and fruit.

"At 10:20, just before I texted you," Monica replied. "She asked if you were in the office. I told her you were at a meeting away from the Questura. She just said to tell you about the funeral and ask if you were coming. She thought you'd want to know."

"That's all? Nothing else?"

"No. Do you want the number?"

"Text it to me. I think I have it, but we haven't talked in a long time. I don't know if she has my cell phone number. Maybe that's why she called the Questura. She knows where I work."

"Oh," Monica said, slightly surprised. "I see. Will you go?"

"I have to. But it couldn't have come at a worse time. This is a very hectic week. And Napoli is, well, Napoli. The last place I want to go."

Monica knew Napoli was Antonella's hometown but didn't under-stand why she wouldn't want to travel there. She had worked for Antonella for three years but knew little of her past or personal life.

Antonella made her way to the table where DIGOS *(Divisione Investigazioni Generali e Operazioni Speciali)* agents were talking or texting, working at computers, and sipping caffè. She sat next to Simona De Monti, one of her top agents, who was texting on her mobile. After only two years in the male-dominated DIGOS, De Monti had earned the reputation of a determined and aggressive investigator, suffering head wounds when her DIGOS colleagues had killed three Muslim terrorists at the La Scala Opera House during the season premiere in December 2013.

De Monti looked up from her phone.

"Bad news, Simo," Antonella said. "I have to leave immediately for Napoli."

De Monti blinked. "Napoli? Why? What's in Napoli?"

Antonella looked around at the DIGOS agents who had noticed that something had disturbed their boss.

"A funeral, totally unexpected." She related Monica's message to De Monti, leaning toward her ear for privacy. De Monti nodded as she heard the details.

"I'm sorry, *dottoressa*. Terrible news. It must be a shock for you," Simona said.

Antonella nodded, noticing that the agents at their table had stopped texting and talking and were staring at her. "Not really—I knew I'd get that call one day."

"You did? But I thought—"

She cut her off. "You don't know the whole story, Simo. Only Giorgio does. You overheard us one day talking about the . . . situation. I didn't go into the gory details, but I will when I return from Napoli."

Simona looked at her, remembering the morning when she'd gone to Antonella's office for a meeting. As she was about to enter, she overheard a snippet of conversation between Antonella and Giorgio Lucchini, the *capo* of DIGOS in Milano.

Antonella had said, "I'm sure he was murdered, dumped someplace. It's been almost a year."

"It's Napoli; you're probably right," Lucchini had replied.

Antonella gasped when she saw Simona in the doorway.

Lucchini turned around, saw her, and stood. He cleared his throat and said, "I'll come back later." He walked out of the office without greeting Simona.

"I'm sorry, *dottoressa*," Simona apologized. "I didn't see Dottor Lucchini. You asked me to come at eleven."

"I did; you're a little early," she said, glancing at her watch. "Lucchini was passing by. I heard some news I wanted to share with him. Nothing that concerns you or the office."

"Are you OK?" Simona asked. "You look pale. Are you going to faint?"

"No, no, I'm fine. Just a little bug I got a few days ago."

De Monti recalled the strange event, embarrassed that she had interrupted superior officers and overheard something neither wanted to talk about. Was that incident, the suspected murder case, related to Amoruso's need to go to Napoli for a funeral? She wasn't going to ask.

"I'll just be gone a few days," Antonella said. "I'll come back as soon as I can." She opened her briefing book to scan the schedule of presentations for the day. Panels on bomb-sniffing dogs, metal detectors at entrances, surveillance inside the Expo, and undercover agents assigned to politically sensitive pavilions—the US, France, Germany, Saudi Arabia, Iran, Afghanistan, China, and Russia being the most obvious.

Antonella pointed to the page with the upcoming panel's presenters. "Simo, can you take my place on the next panel, 'Undercover Surveillance'?"

"Of course, *dottoressa*. I've been to surveillance briefings at the Questura."

"The Carabinieri and Polizia di Stato are leading the panel," said Antonella. "Just be on the platform representing DIGOS, and ask a couple of questions. You can handle it."

"Anything else, *dottoressa?*"

"Write a memo after the panel, and post it on our secure website."

"I will. Dottor Lucchini's in Roma today, isn't he?"

Antonella nodded. "Yes, today and tomorrow, briefings on the refugee crisis in Sicilia. Two more leaking boats coming from Libya capsized last week; more than four hundred died." Antonella glanced at her watch. "I'll text Lucchini that I have to go to Napoli when I'm on the train to Cadorna Station. I don't want a car to drive me into town this time of day."

"For sure, it could take more than an hour with all the road construction."

"Call if anything comes up."

Antonella left her briefing book on the DIGOS table, picked up her purse, and made her way toward the exit. She stopped by the Carabinieri and Guardia di Finanza tables to tell the commanders she had to leave because of an emergency and that Ispettrice De Monti would take her place for the rest of the day.

Antonella signed out at the security desk, left her Expo security badge, and hurried toward the tunnels that would take her to the express train back to Cadorna Station. When she reached the Expo metro station, she called Monica.

"Leaving Expo, going to my apartment. Book a flight to Napoli this evening with my personal credit card, returning Friday afternoon."

The Trenord express train screeched into the Expo station with six new yellow-and-green cars, part of a fleet manufactured for the Expo. Antonella entered an empty car and took a seat as passengers on the platform, businessmen carrying briefcases and Expo employees returning to Milano, entered other cars.

As the train sped away, Antonella called her husband, Carlo, who was flying from Dubai to Sydney that morning. She got his voicemail and left a message. Carlo wouldn't hear her message for several hours; his flight to Sydney was at least sixteen hours long.

Her second call was to her sister, Marianna, who was in Cambridge, Massachusetts, completing a teaching course at Harvard on Giotto, Tintoretto, and Raphael. Antonella calculated that it was six hours earlier in Cambridge, around five in the morning. She left a voicemail telling Marianna she would be on an evening plane to Napoli and why.

Next, Antonella texted her boss, Giorgio Lucchini, about the reason for her flight to Napoli that night. Then she left a voicemail for her maid, telling her not to fix dinner and that she would be gone for a few days.

Antonella pondered calling her sister-in-law, Carmela, who had left the message with Monica at the Questura. They had never been close, the distance growing as Carmela's family had become immersed in the world of the brutal Camorra crime syndicate. Antonella was a distinguished Italian police officer at DIGOS, but her half-brother, Salvatore, was a member of the "honored society" of Camorra.

Antonella took a deep breath and pressed in Carmela's mobile number. The call went immediately to voicemail—not a surprise. Antonella left a message saying she was flying in that night and would go to their apartment tomorrow.

When Antonella arrived at her apartment in Porta Venezia, she went into her bedroom, dropped her purse on the bed, and opened her closet to finger racks of casual, business, and formal wear. She chose the appropriate wardrobe for the hot and muggy weather in Napoli, layered the clothing in her suitcase, and went into the bathroom to retrieve toiletry and cosmetic bags she kept under the sink for traveling.

Her cell phone rang. Monica.

"*Dottoressa,* I booked a seat for the 5:45 p.m. Alitalia flight from Linate, arriving at Capodichino at 7:05 p.m."

"Book me a rental car and a room at the International Hotel."

"Yes, *dottoressa.*"

"Please call everyone on my appointment calendar. Reschedule for next week. Tell them an unexpected event came up and that I'll be out of town. No details other than that."

"Would you like a floral arrangement delivered for the funeral?"

Antonella paused. She would want a floral wreath with her and Carlo's names at the church. But what kind of arrangement? The traditional, with bouquets of lilies? What message? Too much to think about now. Later.

"No. I'll arrange it in Napoli."

After packing, Antonella took a shower, slipped on her bathrobe, went back into her bedroom, and reached for the TV remote. She was rarely at her apartment during the day and never watched TV, but she needed a distraction.

She clicked through Rai 1, Rai 2, Rai Premium, Mediaset, 24-hour news . . . endless commercials, vapid hostesses, newscasters who looked like movie stars reading news off of teleprompters. They weren't journalists, only stylish readers. A waste of time. She clicked off the TV and tossed the remote onto her bed.

Antonella went into the kitchen and opened the refrigerator. She hadn't had lunch, only a cappuccino before the morning briefing. She grabbed plastic-wrapped asiago cheese, prosciutto slices, and tomatoes, layering them on slices of artisanal bread for a quick lunch.

She returned to her bedroom, feeling more settled now that arrangements had been made. She picked up her phone and called for a taxi to pick her up at 3:45 p.m.

Flight. Hotel. Rental car. Taxi to the airport. Done.

She had rushed that morning to get home and pack, and now she had unexpected time on her hands. Her days were rigidly structured, but today she was home with a couple of hours to kill until the taxi arrived. What to do?

Antonella reached for a stack of books on her nightstand. She occasionally tried to read before going to sleep, never staying awake for more than ten minutes. The last book she had finished was Elena Ferrante's *My Brilliant Friend,* about two young Neapolitan girls growing up in a seedy neighborhood after World War II. Before she started book 2 in Ferrante's series, she wanted to try another author who also wrote about Napoli. She picked up *Neapolitan Chronicles* by Anna Maria Ortese, a journalist who wrote short stories and memoirs about Napoli in the 1950s and 1960s. Not happy stories—tales of struggle and sadness for families like hers after the war. She stuffed it into her suitcase.

Antonella had ventured far from Napoli in her personal and professional life. But her hometown, a city influenced by the Greeks, Arabs, Spanish, and French, retained a hold on her childhood memories of growing up in that odd and dangerous historic city. Vesuvio, the legendary volcano located just 9 kilometers east of Napoli, had a strange grip on her imagination as a little girl. When she'd see the two peaks, she imagined they looked like two kittens snuggled under a green rug. Later, she thought of a woman lying on her side, the higher peak her hips, the lower, her shoulders.

When she understood the tectonic threat of Vesuvio, she'd watch columns of smoke rising from the caldera in fascination, fearing that it was about to erupt as it had in 79 AD, burying Pompei and Ercolano in mounds of molten lava and ash, and killing thousands. She asked her parents, who were both teachers, about the dangers of living so close to an active volcano. Her childish imagination of kittens and a woman became nightmares until she was a teenager.

Antonella had loved Napoli as a child; it was her hometown, filled with friends, neighbors, and family. But as she grew up, she experienced the dark side of her hometown, its depravity and crime. She never understood why people would pickpocket, break into a home, or steal a car or motorcycle. What would they gain from committing a crime? It was wrong. Crime hurt people. Looking back years later, she supposed that belief was why she chose a career with the police, to wage a personal crusade against crime. Even though Antonella was now an adult, Napoli maintained its grip on her emotions and memories. Mezzogiorno and Napoli were in her blood. They were part of her life.

Antonella sat on her bed looking up at a bookshelf with framed black-and-white photos of her family. She got up, walked barefoot to the bookshelf, and picked up a photo: Antonella when she was nine years old, wearing a white lace dress, a tiara, and white gloves for her first communion. Her seven-year-old sister, Marianna, stood alongside her, beaming at her older sister. Their father and mother stood proudly behind the girls.

Antonella put the photo down and picked up a second one: two years later, Marianna's first communion. She was wearing the same white lace dress, tiara, and gloves. Antonella stood next to Marianna, wearing a blue dress and white shoes. Their parents were again behind them.

Their father had aged from the first photo, looking older than forty-six, his small mouth pinched like he was in pain, eyes tired and sad. His black hair was mussed, beige shirt wrinkled, tie loose at his neck. Their mother had gained weight, a soft bulge around her waist, arms stretching the sleeves of her black dress, her feet cramped in dusty brown shoes.

A third photo: Antonella was thirteen, Marianna eleven, on holiday with the family at a Capri beach. It was the first family photo with their half-brother, Salvatore, seventeen years old, who visited the family only on holidays and time off school. Salvatore stood apart from their father, slouching, eyes avoiding the camera.

A fourth photo: at a trattoria in Napoli under the shade of a canopy of grapevines twisting around wooden poles. Salvatore sat at the opposite end of the table, facing his father and stepmother, with his wife, Carmela, on his left, holding their baby, Luisa.

A fifth photo: Salvatore, Carmela, two-year-old Luisa, and baby Diego in front of a church after Diego's baptism.

A modest shrine to her past. Just five photos of her family. None from her father's or mother's funerals. Tonight, she was going back to Napoli for another funeral. But she wouldn't return with photos for her bookshelf. Antonella had no interest in remembering this family gathering. People she didn't know or care to know would snap mobile phone photos and post them on Facebook and Instagram. Some at the funeral would be criminals, morbidly capturing Carmela's family's grief, posting banal comments: "I was there . . . a family mourning . . . those poor children, losing their father."

Antonella rarely felt melancholy, an emotion that seemed mawkish and self-indulgent. It was a waste of time and energy. She needed a distraction, something to get her mind off the past and what was lying ahead.

In an alcove off the dining room, she sat down at her desktop computer, logged into the secure DIGOS site, and scrolled through emails and reports. A security alert from Torino: Suspected arson at a bus terminal, two injured, possible domestic terrorism linked to demonstrations against TAV, the Torino–Lyon high-speed train under the Alps.

An email from Simona with notes from the Expo briefing. Antonella checked her schedule for the week ahead of meetings coordinating Expo security details. Tomorrow, De Monti and other DIGOS colleagues would be at working sessions with the Polizia di Stato and the Guardia di Finanza at the Questura; the next day, they'd be on to Carabinieri headquarters for more Expo meetings.

At 3 p.m. Lucchini called.

"*Ciao,* Antonella. Sorry I couldn't call earlier—morning meetings, lunch presentations, a working dinner tonight. I'm sorry about the funeral in Napoli. A sad time for you and the family. Please accept my condolences."

"Thank you, Giorgio. We've talked about this; we both knew this would happen sometime. I just have to get through the week. I'm packed, leaving for Linate soon. How are your meetings?"

He exhaled a long sigh. She could almost see his face: brow wrinkled, eyes narrowed in frustration. "Long day, watching gruesome videos of refugees on leaking boats, bodies in the water, babies dead in their mothers' arms. Those poor people are harmless, victims of criminals extorting them to get on unsafe boats, knowing they'll die. Our navy and coast guard are lucky to save a few if they reach the boats before they sink."

"Life is cruel, especially if you're from Africa or the Middle East," Antonella said.

"How long will you be in Napoli?" he asked, changing the subject.

"I'll be back Friday afternoon and go to the office Saturday to catch up. The timing couldn't be worse . . . riots and burning cars Friday, and who knows what might happen this week. God, I hate to go. I want to stay, but—"

"You have to go, Antonella," Lucchini interrupted. "It's your family; they need you in Napoli. I'm confident our police forces will be able to handle any problems. We anticipated demonstrators creating chaos, and they were ready. They'll be prepared this week also. Go to Napoli."

"All right, I know that. It's just that—"

"Go. That's it," Lucchini emphasized. "I'll see you Saturday. You'll be gone only a few days. Other than the funeral and seeing Salvo's family, what else will you do?"

"A few things. I'll go to the Pianura police station and see Commissario Belmondo. He can brief me on the details. I'm not looking forward to it, but I need to know."

"That's up to you. I know this will all be difficult for you. Will you do anything else?"

"I'll look up an old friend or two and spend time with my niece and nephew. I haven't seen them for two years. They're teenagers now. You know how critical those years are. Teenagers face peer pressures—clothes, friends, social life. But Napoli teenagers are lured into crime. Petty stuff at first—pickpocketing, stealing, telling addicts where they can get drugs. But soon they're into serious crimes like selling drugs, burglaries, stealing cars, even murder."

"You know it well—Napoli has the highest number of youth murder convictions in the country," Lucchini said. "Eighteen, nineteen, twenty years old, and they end up in prison, where they get raped and beaten as soon as the doors slam behind them."

Antonella shuddered. "The police, churches, and schools have failed. Camorra families have been criminals for generations. Children in those families don't know any other life. I worry about Luisa and Diego. I don't hear from them. Their mother and I don't talk. She doesn't trust me because I'm a cop."

"All the more reason for you to be there. Show them there are alternatives to being *camorristi*. They need you."

"Yes, they do. But . . . to be completely honest, I'm dreading going. Many of the people I'll meet will be *camorristi*. They'll know I'm a cop."

"Are you worried?"

She thought for a moment. "Yes, I am, a little. But I have to go."

"Be careful."

CHAPTER TWO

When the taxi arrived, Antonella took her suitcase down in the elevator and instructed the driver to take her to the airport.

At Linate airport, she passed through a special door marked *Security Personnel—Restricted*. She showed her DIGOS identification and the 9mm Beretta in her belt holster to a police official. The official examined her identification, made a copy, and had her sign a logbook.

"When you get on the plane, ask to see the pilot and show him your DIGOS identification. Pilots have final approval for passengers carrying a weapon, but it's just routine."

Antonella entered the security area and joined passengers moving toward their gates. She boarded the plane and told the attendant she wanted to see the pilot, stepping aside to let passengers move down the aisle to their seats.

The pilot—a senior pilot judging by the epaulets on his uniform—emerged from the cockpit.

"*Buona sera*. They told me you were flying with us tonight," he said, smiling at Antonella. He glanced at her DIGOS identification. She lifted her coat to show her holstered Beretta. "No problem, *dottoressa*. We welcome police on our flights. Take your seat, and enjoy the flight. It will be smooth flying all the way to Napoli."

Antonella took her seat in the third row, next to the window. She locked her seat belt and listened as the flight attendant droned through the pre-departure checklist.

When the plane departed the gate, Antonella gazed out the window. She was looking forward to the flight, with no phones, no conversation, just time alone to relax and reflect. The day had been a disruption, coming to an end on an airplane instead of at the office or at home—not what she ever could have expected when she'd left her apartment that morning. But there was nothing she could do; she was on her way to Napoli, anxious about what would come in the next few days.

It would be a reunion of sorts with Carmela and her family, whom she had not seen in two years. That experience had been unpleasant— even gruesome—for all. The day she arrived, the family was somber but hopeful that Salvo would return home after he'd been missing for four days. The next morning, two police officers arrived while the children were at school. They told Carmela and Antonella they had information from an undercover source that Salvo had possibly been murdered.

Antonella didn't want to dwell on the painful memory of her last trip to Napoli. She gazed out the window as her plane wheeled toward the runway to wait in line to take off. Flying was usually a pleasure for her; Carlo worked in the industry, and they had flown on many flights for memorable holidays to exotic locations.

She leaned back and relaxed, recalling pleasant memories of her childhood in Napoli—her mother hugging her and Marianna when they left for school in the morning, walking to school, her classroom with Sister Domenica, friends she had since lost touch with, the first boy who kissed her . . . Carmine De Vivo. Where was he today? Was Carmine as handsome and charming as when they first embraced and shared a passionate kiss on Capri beach one sultry August evening? A week later, Antonella had witnessed Carmine embrace and kiss another girl at a café near their school. When he opened his eyes, he saw Antonella watching from across the street. She turned away, never letting Carmine try to explain. Her heart was broken. How could a boy who had whispered soothing words of love and care while he embraced her, running his hands over her back and rear, betray her days later?

She tried to hide her tears as she ran home, hiding from her mother when she came into the apartment, racing into her bedroom, slamming the door, and falling on the bed, sobbing. When Mamma opened the door, Antonella hid her face, waved her mother away.

"No, Mamma, leave me alone, please . . . I saw Carmine kiss another girl! How could he? Why would he do that? I loved him . . . why would he do that?"

Antonella chuckled at the memory. The emotions of a teenage Neapolitan girl were as volatile as Vesuvio, smoldering day and night, and then erupting in dramatic, fiery explosions that lit up the sky. Yes, that was her; she had erupted that day. The next morning after school, when Carmine was waiting for her, she pushed him away, hissing, "Never talk to me again. Never come to my school again. I never want to see you again. Never. Never!" He obeyed.

What a satisfying memory, refusing to let Carmine talk to her after he had betrayed her. She was so young and innocent but had learned a valuable lesson in life's realities. People betray you. People you trust. The lesson: Be careful who you allow to enter your life. There are a lot of Carmines out there.

Antonella didn't kiss another boy until Luigi Fusco came into her life in her senior year. Luigi was two years older, an economics student at the *Università degli Studi di Napoli*. After a few casual dates, coffees, and meeting his friends, she felt she could trust him. He was no Carmine. He was a gentleman, thoughtful and considerate. And he kept his word. If he promised to meet her at 3 p.m., he was ten minutes early. He took her home when she asked him to. He was respectful, a bit shy around her mother, who later told Antonella that he was a nice young man. She knew about Carmine and said Luigi was not like him.

* * * * *

The day after Antonella's eighteenth birthday party, Luigi took her out to dinner and for a walk around the Posillipo peninsula at dusk. A full moon was shining on the Bay of Napoli. He kissed her, the first of many kisses. A month later, they slept together, her first time. They were lovers for three years, a happy time for Antonella, and she was eager to experience the joys of a first love. She confided to Luigi her dream of having a career as a lawyer, earning a comfortable income, renting a nice apartment in Roma. Getting married. Having children. Raising a family. Luigi wanted to marry her, to be the father of their children, to live in Roma with her after he graduated from university.

It was not to be. He never joined her in Roma. His studies led him to an advanced degree at Bocconi University in Milano. Antonella was sad, but she understood. Luigi was an intellectual, always studying, reading technical books, a man whose brain never stopped humming.

In her early twenties, while she was studying in Roma, Antonella experienced other personal disappointments, twists, turns, diversions, and collisions with brick walls. By the time she received her law degree, Luigi was working in Brussels as an economist with the Italian finance ministry. And married with a child. Instead of pursuing a job with a law firm, Antonella applied to become a police officer in Roma.

She was accepted, trained for a year, patrolled the streets of Roma in a police car, and was promoted to become a Polizia di Stato investigator.

Where was Luigi today? She didn't know and didn't really care; their affair was in the distant past. She had had many lovers after Luigi. Where was Raffaele Liguori, her lover when she patrolled Roma's streets at twenty-seven? Antonella smiled; she would always remember Raffaele with warm thoughts and best wishes. Feeling the gentle pulsing of the plane in flight, she closed her eyes but didn't want to sleep. She wanted to relax and not worry about what was to come.

The flight was uneventful except for a wave of bumps and dips as the plane crossed the Apennines and flew west of Pisa, a few miles from the Ligurian coastline and the ink-blue Mediterranean Sea. The sun, low in the western sky, blazed through the starboard windows, illuminating the cabin.

* * * * *

When her flight landed at Capodichino and rolled to the gate, Antonella exited the plane and wheeled her suitcase through the air-conditioned terminal into Napoli's hot, muggy evening air. She caught a shuttle bus to the International Hotel, checked in, pulled her suitcase into the elevator, and punched the button for the sixth floor. A *whoosh* vibrated the elevator all the way to her floor, as she stood with one hand on the rail, the other gripping her suitcase handle. Antonella exited, walked to the end of the corridor, slipped the key card into the slot, and entered her room.

Standard, neutral business-hotel décor: beige carpet, pastel yellow walls, framed pictures of Napoli and the Amalfi Coast. A desk, a large-screen TV, and a boxy refrigerator in a cabinet. Fluffy white duvet, three pale-blue pillows, and a plastic card on the bed for ordering from the restaurant. She tossed her purse and suitcase onto the bed and went to the window, throwing back the curtains and stepping out onto the balcony.

Napoli at dusk. Long rows of streetlights flickered along wide avenues along Napoli's sweeping bay. A ribbon of clouds hung over Vesuvio's jagged caldera, which looked like a humpbacked blister bathed in the glow of the rising moon. Mute, menacing, dormant. Who knew when it would erupt again, spewing molten magma and poisonous gases into Napoli suburbs, smothering them in burning ash and pumice like Pompei in 79 AD? The volcano still had a powerful hold on her imagination but didn't give her nightmares anymore, thank God. However, at the strangest times, without any connections or hints, she would picture it her mind, looming, beautiful but dangerous. A memory of her younger life that would always be a part of her. Massive. Threatening. Unforgettable.

* * * * *

Antonella looked down, her attention drawn by a tinkle of laughter and splashing from below. She saw guests reclining on lounge chairs and sat at tables with umbrellas around an oval-shaped swimming pool with three lap lanes. Children were splashing in the shallow end. A slim woman in a red swimsuit was swimming laps, executing flip turns. Antonella wondered if the woman's life was one of leisure—yoga, lap swimming, spas, and beauty treatments.

When the woman finished her laps, a man with long dark hair emerged from under an umbrella and handed her a towel. She climbed the ceramic tile steps, grabbed the towel, and ruffled it through her damp hair. She wrapped the towel around herself, took the man's hand, and followed him under the umbrella. A waiter came over, nodded at them, and turned back, probably taking a drink order. Two Camparis, likely.

Antonella couldn't see the woman's face as she was swimming or when hidden under the umbrella, just her long, tanned legs. Antonella fantasized about the swimmer: enjoying a relaxing swim after a sultry day in Napoli, a handsome man waiting on her, sipping drinks by the pool, making love that night.

Antonella's phone rang. She dashed into the room. Marianna.

"*Buona sera*, Marianna," she said. "No, it's afternoon for you, evening here."

"It's going on 3 p.m. in Boston. I just got out of a lecture. Where are you?"

"Napoli. I just checked in at the hotel."

"Why are you there?"

"Salvo was our half-brother, Marianna."

"But he was a *camorrista*, a criminal, and you're a cop!" she protested. "He went to jail. More than once. Maybe he even murdered someone."

"No, Marianna," Antonella said. "He wasn't a murderer; he was just involved in selling drugs. And yes, he was a criminal."

"You would have arrested him if you were a cop in Napoli."

"I might have, but I'm not. I hated what he did and told him many times. You know how much he and I argued about his criminal activities."

"Yeah, and look what good it did. What about the time he almost killed you on a Vespa?"

Antonella sighed. Marianna always brought up this very unfortunate accident when Antonella had been a naïve ten-year-old.

"Yes, that happened, but I just ended up with broken ribs and a couple scars." Antonella pressed a hand on the left side of her rib cage, where faint scars could still be seen when she took off her blouse: three jagged lines that looked like they were traced with a red ink pen. "I was lucky, no doubt about it."

"He *stole* the Vespa, Antonella! Took you for a ride! Without helmets. And then he wrecked it! He almost killed you. He was a criminal at fourteen! Remember how mad Mamma and Papà were?"

"I do. I do," Antonella said, recalling that August afternoon Salvo was coming to spend the weekend before school resumed. He showed up riding a new Vespa, yellow and shiny, not a scratch or smudge, as if it had just come off the dealer's display floor.

"Hop on the back, Nelluccia!" Salvo had yelled when he saw her on the street. "Let's have some fun!"

And they did. They left Soccavo, sped into Napoli, raced up steep hills, and skidded over cobblestone streets, scaring pedestrians, cats, and dogs. When Salvo turned corners, Antonella screamed and closed her eyes, gripping his belly. When she opened her eyes, her hair swirled around like a tornado. It was thrilling, racing up and down Napoli's narrow, hilly streets, speeding between parked and moving cars. When she wasn't laughing, she was screaming at the excitement.

Then it happened.

A car in front of them braked to a sudden stop, forcing Salvo to jerk the handlebars. The Vespa slammed into a curb and crashed into a parked car. Salvo flew over the handlebars, head over heels, landing on his stomach on the street.

Antonella slammed into the hood of the car and collapsed on the street.

It was over in a split second—the most terrifying event in Antonella's young life. She woke up in a hospital in excruciating pain, with broken ribs, a cracked nose, black eyes, and swollen lips. Salvo, she learned later, had suffered a black eye, multiple bruises, and gashes on his cheek and forehead.

After the accident, Antonella didn't see Salvo for months; he was banished from the family home by their father. The next time she saw him, he was no longer the happy-go-lucky, fun-seeking, crazy half-brother. He was embittered by his first arrest, charged with stealing the Vespa. Their father made him work to pay off the owner for the wrecked Vespa. Salvo dropped out of school to work as an apprentice mechanic. He never returned.

"Sure, Salvo was our half-brother," Marianna said, "but he was a criminal who wanted nothing to do with us."

"But he has a family—Carmela, Luisa, and Diego. I want to be there for them. Maybe I can help them."

"How? Not with money; they don't need money! You know that. Camorra takes care of families when someone is jailed or murdered."

"Not money. Just show them I care about them. This may be one of the last times I come to Napoli."

"I won't go back. My life is far better than anything I could have had in Napoli."

"Mine, too. But they're our family—you, me, Carmela, and her children."

Silence on the line. Both had expressed their opinions; neither was going to change their minds or agree with the other. This was a dispute between them that had lasted for decades, one of the few topics they couldn't resolve.

After a minute, Marianna ended the impasse. "All right, Antonella, you've made up your mind," Marianna said with a sigh. "Are you going to buy a wreath for the funeral?"

"Yes, and I'll add your name."

"I'm sorry if I sound so . . . cold, but I'd never do what you're doing."

"Don't be sorry, Marianna. I'm here because I want to be. I'll be home Friday, and this will be all over."

"Call me when you're home. I want to tell you about Cambridge."

"I'll tell Carmela and the children you'll pray for them."

"Oh, yeah, sure, I'll do that."

"Send a card. Write something . . . thoughtful. They need to hear from you."

"OK. Bye. I love you," Marianna said.

"Same here—I'm glad you called."

Antonella dropped the phone onto the bed and went back out to the balcony. She wasn't upset by Marianna's call. Marianna had never been close to Salvo. When he came for brief visits, she'd go over to a friend's home or play outside. She didn't like being around him. He'd call her "a baby," and she'd cry. Antonella knew Salvo better before his life turned, when they were just two kids, big half-brother and little half-sister. He incessantly teased her. They were always arguing, sometimes making up before he left and didn't return for weeks. At a young age, Antonella learned important behaviors from Salvo—always stand up for your beliefs, learn how to express yourself when attacked, learn how to fight with words, not fists.

Salvo, unfortunately, had one behavior that defined him: he tried to get his way by being a bully.

If things had been different, maybe . . . maybe Salvo would not have become a criminal. But no one could change the past.

Antonella was tired and ready to go to bed after a long day. She wanted one last look at the sprawling Bay of Napoli, where a flotilla of COSCO and Maersk ships were anchored offshore with white, blue, green, and red containers stacked on their decks like giant Legos.

Inside the shipping containers were manufactured products from Seoul, Shenzhen, Guangzhou, Shanghai, and Taipei, destined for European stores. Every type of toy imaginable, plus jeans, raincoats,

cigarettes, electronics. Designer clothes, shoes, and handbags from
Bangladesh for Armani, Gucci, Prada, and Dolce & Gabbana were also
aboard, with labels that said *Made in Italia.*

Antonella looked back at Vesuvio, silent but deadly, like Napoli
itself, an imposing presence on the coastline of Campania. Vesuvio
was nature's shrine to the volatile tectonic forces that had formed the
earth millions of years ago. Boiling magma simmered below the jagged
caldera, spewing hot, toxic gases through fissure vents, threatening to
erupt, maim, scar, and kill sinners and innocents alike, as it had more
than a dozen times in the eighteenth and nineteenth centuries, as well
as three times in the twentieth century.

The muggy air was cooling. Antonella glanced below at the pool.
The swimmer and her companion emerged from under the umbrella,
a towel tucked around her waist. They walked hand in hand into the
hotel and disappeared. A lone waiter in a white coat wheeled a cart to
the tables, retrieving wineglasses, bottles, paper plates, and napkins.

Antonella was back in her hometown, experiencing waves of melancholy, anxiety, and anticipation. What would happen over the next
few days? She longed for the security and comfort of her Milano home.

She took one last look at the night sky: horsetail clouds over Ischia,
Capri, and the Amalfi Coast; container ships in the bay; Vesuvio in the
moonlight.

Dusk had become night. Napoli would be sleeping soon, but not
Vesuvio. It never slept.

CHAPTER THREE

TUESDAY

Antonella tossed and turned during the night, sheets wrapped around her legs like ropes. She was dreaming she was back in her apartment, frantically searching for the keys to her family's home that she had taken back to Milano after her mother's funeral.

Antonella was opening dresser drawers, throwing contents around her bedroom, opening shoe boxes and shopping bags in her closet, turning over mattresses, lifting up carpets. She had put the keys in a "safe" place but couldn't remember where that safe place was.

The key ring was a steel band with three keys; one for the outer gate, a second to enter the building, a third to the apartment. It was more than a set of keys; it was a family heirloom. Antonella's grandfather had welded a red Italian military medal to the key ring he carried in his coat pocket when he left for work. He'd received the medal for fighting the Nazis when the Allied armies approached Napoli in September 1943. At the end of each day, he hung the key ring on a wooden rack, another heirloom, by the door.

* * * * *

Every family in her Soccavo neighborhood had similar key racks carved by Ricardo, an old man crippled from a German grenade during the liberation of Napoli. The grenade had been tossed into Ricardo's home, severely wounding him and killing his wife and two children. A dent in his right temple from shrapnel had damaged Ricardo's brain and left him barely able to talk or walk. Over the years, Ricardo struggled to survive, carving wooden stools, chairs, tables, toys, and key racks that he sold for a few hundred lire.

Antonella would see Ricardo when she walked to school in the morning, sitting on one of his handmade wooden stools, surrounded by the mewing feral cats he fed and watered from wooden bowls he'd carved.

One morning, Ricardo wasn't on his stool. When Antonella returned home that afternoon, her mother told her the old man had died. The next week, workmen tore down his home—a shack with a leaky roof, broken cement doorsteps, and cracked windows. The workmen erected a chain fence around the small lot. Ricardo's house was rubble; all that remained were feral cats, mewing for water and food.

Antonella awoke from her dream, hearing the flutter of the gauzy curtains caught in the breeze coming through the opening she had left in the sliding balcony window when she'd gone to bed. She preferred fresh air when she slept, not stale, dead air from closed-up windows in apartments and hotels.

She listened to the curtains fluttering, her foggy brain drifting back to her dream, head nestled in her pillow, body wrapped in damp sheets.

She glanced at the digital clock by her bed. 6:12. Antonella picked up her phone and turned it on to check messages. One voicemail, four texts. She read the texts, smiled at the one from Carlo: *Cara, call me when you're awake. Love you, sorry about the news.*

It was too early to call anyone, even Carlo. She had to clear out the fog from her brain.

She retreated into the bathroom, feeling the cool ceramic tiles on the soles of her feet. She tugged her nightgown over her head, turned on the shower, and let streams of warm water flow through her fingers. When it was the right temperature, she stepped in, rotating slowly to let hot water soothe her wakening body.

After her shower, Antonella slipped on a terrycloth robe hanging behind the door and wrapped a towel around her damp hair. She flipped open her suitcase and pulled out underwear, slacks, a blouse, and sandals. When she was dressed with her hair combed, she called Carlo in Australia. He answered after two rings.

"*Buongiorno, cara.* How are you?"

"Oh, it's so nice to hear your voice, Carlo. I miss you, wish you were here."

"When did you get to Napoli?"

"Last night. I'm at the International Hotel."

"Wonderful. I know the manager, Vincenzo. Mention my name; he'll upgrade you to a suite."

"No, no. I'm fine." She related the events from the previous day, getting Monica's text, leaving the Expo, returning home to pack, and taking a taxi to Linate.

"Do you want me to join you? I could leave tonight."

"Of course not. You just got to Sydney. How was your flight?"

"First class is the only way to endure long flights. I don't see how people survive flying coach. I managed to sleep a couple hours, but the flight was a little rough—some kind of storm over the Indian Ocean."

"I worry about you flying all the time."

"Don't. Air travel is very safe."

"Unless you fly Malaysian Airlines." She bit her lip; it was the wrong thing to say. Carlo was an airline executive. Why bring up those tragic Malaysian flights? One disappeared in the Indian Ocean in 2014, the second was shot down in the same year by Russian artillery in Ukraine. "I'm sorry—that wasn't nice," she apologized. "Forget what I said."

Carlo sensed that Antonella's comment about airline safety had more to do with her state of mind than being sarcastic. Being in Napoli for a family funeral would be stressful. When Antonella was under pressure such as this, she had bad dreams and woke up anxious and exhausted. He considered asking her about how she'd slept but then decided to change the subject.

"When is the funeral?"

"Thursday morning. I haven't talked to Carmela yet. She doesn't answer her phone; she thinks it's tapped by DIGOS. She texted last night, asked me to come to the apartment this morning. Luisa will be there."

"You like Luisa, don't you?"

"I do; she's a sweet girl. Last time I saw her, she was fourteen. I imagine she's grown up quite a bit."

"Have you talked to Marianna?"

"Yes, last night. She was upset that I came. She never forgot how Salvo treated her as a child, mocking her, calling her bad names. Not to mention his affiliation with the *sistema*."

"So, you'll be alone. No husband or sister at the funeral. Will you be OK?"

"I'll manage. It's only a few days. I'll be home Friday. What are you doing in Sydney today?"

They chatted for ten minutes, a welcome interlude before she started her day. After she hung up with Carlo, Antonella texted Lucchini to tell him she was going to the family's apartment and then to the Pianura police department. She answered Carmela's text, telling her she would go to her apartment soon.

Lucchini texted back when she was in the elevator: "Meetings all day, call me tonight."

Antonella sipped a cappuccino and nibbled a brioche in the hotel café; then she went to the concierge to pick up her rental car.

"All arranged, Dottoressa Amoruso," the concierge said. "A valet will drive it from the garage. Here's the paperwork."

Five minutes later, Antonella was behind the steering wheel of a black Fiat Punto. She turned the air conditioning on full blast to combat the muggy morning heat and eased into the congestion of commuters driving in from outlying suburbs and trailer trucks departing from the wharf loaded down with containers from ships.

Streams of slow-moving cars, buses, and trailer trucks inched along the Autostrada A56. Most annoying were motorcycles speeding between cars and trucks, spewing noxious black exhaust that seeped into cars even with the windows up. A56 in central Napoli was a stretch of cement walls covered with graffiti mocking politicians and celebrities. None subtle, most tending toward violence or obscenities: knives dripping with blood, armed weapons firing, bombs exploding, crude pornography, obscenities, slanderous political slogans—often misspelled.

Behind the graffitied walls, rows of apartment and office buildings with billboards on their roofs advertised cell phones, slinky lingerie, lottery tickets, designer handbags, running shoes, cheap flights to Ibiza, Palermo, and Sardegna.

She drove into the Quattro Giornate Tunnel, bored through Napoli's steep hills, and emerged in the bright sunlight of the Fuorigrotta neighborhood of high-rise apartments. Minutes later, she passed a road sign for Soccavo—where she grew up—and was soon driving past cheap furniture warehouses, used-car dealers, roadside plant vendors, and fake Napoli soccer uniforms.

She exited into Pianura, a lower-class area developed by shady companies with Camorra connections, who ignored Napoli's bureaucratic process of filing real estate permits and inspections. The result was unsightly—remnants of old farms and stone fences covered in weeds, pot-holed streets, crumbling curbs, and shabby apartments. It was garbage-pickup day in Pianura, which meant overflowing green and blue bins clustered on street corners, in alleys, and on empty lots. Torn plastic bags and busted paper sacks had attracted feral cats, mangy dogs, and crows that picked through the trash.

When she reached Carmela's apartment on Via Evangelista Torricelli, she parked and walked past apartments with clusters of satellite dishes on rooftops, barred windows on bottom floors, and posters of the democratic party, Forza Italia, Beppe Grillo's anti-establishment Five Star Movement, and a Napoli soccer match.

Antonella scanned the apartment directory, a list of initials of family names: Carmela's apartment was SC, Salvatore and Carmela. She was about to press the SC button when the front door opened. A young mother carrying a baby in a sling came out and held the door open for Antonella.

She walked down a hallway to the elevator and pressed the call button. Moments later, the thud of the elevator signaled its arrival on the ground floor. She opened the metal gate, squeezed inside the cramped cage, and pressed the fourth-floor button.

The elevator rose, gently bumping as it passed floors. When it stopped, Antonella exited, walked to the end of a corridor, and knocked on Carmela's door.

Tap tap tap. No response. She tapped again, hearing music from a stringed instrument coming from inside. A violin?

The music stopped, and she heard a faint shuffle behind the door. A childlike voice asked, "Who is it?"

"Luisa, it's Zia Antonella."

An inside lock clicked. A second click. The door opened a crack, the metal latch still in place. Two dark eyes with long eyelashes peeked out.

"*Buongiorno*, Luisa. I arrived last night. Did your mother tell you?"

"Oh, I'm so glad you're here, Zia. I've been waiting. Just a moment." The door closed, a latch was removed.

When the door swung open, Luisa fell into Antonella's arms.

"Oh, Zia, Zia, I can't tell you how happy I am to see you."

Luisa pressed her slim body into Antonella's as if she wanted to melt into her. Antonella nestled Luisa's head into her chest, kissing her forehead and smoothing a hand over Luisa's curly hair.

"I've missed you, Luisa, and couldn't wait to see you. I'm sorry about your father. I can't imagine how sad you are."

"Oh, yes—I feel so bad about everything. But you're here now." Luisa pulled back; she took Antonella's hand. "Let's go inside, Zia. Mamma's not home. Would you like *caffè*, water?"

"No, I'm fine."

"Let's sit on the couch so we can talk."

Antonella glanced at Luisa as they walked toward the sofa. She had matured, becoming a beautiful teenager with intense, dark eyes, upturned nose, and a perfect complexion, smooth and unblemished, like porcelain. Much more attractive than anemic models in fashion magazines posing with slouching postures, sour pouts, and hair rumpled as if they had just rolled out of bed. She was a young woman now, with curled eyelashes and wearing makeup—dark-red lipstick and mascara. For a moment, Antonella felt she was looking in a mirror, back to when she was sixteen—but Antonella hadn't worn cosmetics.

Luisa led her to a leather sofa alongside a glass table covered with teen magazines, sports newspapers, two iPads, cell-phone chargers, a TV remote, and an ashtray.

They sat down. Luisa nestled close to Antonella, continuing to hold her hand.

"There's so much to tell you, Zia. It's so lonely without Papà here, and then we find out he was murdered . . . *murdered!*" Luisa sobbed, her words spilling out in a flood of emotion and pain. "Why would anyone want to kill Papà? He was a good father; I miss him so much. I don't know what to do. Hold me, please."

Antonella put her arm around her, squeezed her, feeling Luisa trembling like a young tree in a storm.

She kissed Luisa's forehead. "I'll help any way I can, Luisa. You know I will."

"Oh, I want you to," she pleaded, sniffling. "We need you, Zia . . . You're strong. Stronger than anyone I know."

Antonella was puzzled. What did Luisa mean, "stronger than anyone I know"? She'd had limited contact with the family and hadn't been to Napoli in two years. Unsure how to respond, she continued smoothing her hand over Luisa's head.

"Just before he . . . disappeared two years ago, Papà and Diego were arguing. He told Diego, 'Don't get in trouble, or you'll have to deal with someone like Zia Antonella one day. She won't let you get away with *nothing*,'" Luisa said.

Antonella was stunned. Salvo had been caustic in the limited contact they'd had over the last several years. Why would he praise her in front of his children and be critical to her face?

"He did?" Antonella asked, regretting it as soon as the words came out.

"Whenever he and Diego were fighting, he'd tell him about you being a police officer. And you are, aren't you?"

"Yes."

"I tell my friends you are. They ask me how you become a police officer."

Antonella could not believe what Luisa was saying. She couldn't imagine that teenagers in Napoli would have an interest in becoming police. She had no idea how to respond.

"Can you help the police find out who killed Papà?"

"No, I can't. The local police investigate crimes in Pianura."

"Yeah, Mamma told me, but I wanted to ask."

"I can help in other ways, Luisa; tell me what you need."

Luisa raised her head, pushed back, wiped tears from her cheeks.

"Just be here . . . talk to me. Mamma's depressed, really depressed, since the police found Papà. She didn't come home from work until midnight last night, so Diego and I ate leftover pizza," she said and pointed toward the dining-room table, cluttered with plates of pizza crusts, bottles of olive oil and vinegar, wooden salt and pepper shakers, and a corked wine bottle. "I know she drank too much after her shift was over."

"You didn't go to school today?"

Luisa shook her head.

"Mamma said I could stay home this week. The funeral's Thursday; we see Father Vincenzo tomorrow. Mamma's brother and sister-in-law are coming, too. We don't see them much; they live in Palermo. He's older than Mamma. He's been sick a lot."

"I understand; it would be difficult to go to school with all of this going on. I'm so sorry, Luisa."

"How long will you be here, Zia?"

"I go back Friday."

"Oh. I thought you might stay longer. Where are you staying?"

"At the International Hotel near Capodichino," she said, relieved that she wouldn't be invited to stay at Carmela's apartment. She wouldn't be comfortable spending even one night there.

"Oh, that's good. Mamma's brother and my *zia* are staying in the guest bedroom. They'll be here tonight. They're not bringing their kids; they're spoiled brats."

New information; she didn't know about Carmela's brother or his family.

"How is your mother?" she asked. "This is a very difficult time for her—for all of you."

"It was a shock, even though we knew we'd find out what happened . . ."

Antonella nodded. "I was shocked when I got your mother's message yesterday."

"You know Mamma works at the Vesuvio Pizzeria? She wants you to come tonight for dinner."

"Yes, she texted me the address."

"Diego works at the pizzeria sometimes. He washes dishes, takes out the garbage, sweeps, that kind of stuff. He's only fourteen, but Mamma wants him to do something rather than hang out and get in trouble with other boys. Her boss pays him a few euros each week, so the police don't find out."

"Children can't legally work until they're sixteen."

Luisa laughed. "Yeah, get in trouble hiring an under-age boy. That's not all the trouble they'd be in."

"What do you mean?"

"Zia, you know that Vesuvio is owned by the Rocco family. They sell drugs for the Camorra. You know about them, I'm sure, with you being in the police."

"I do." Antonella didn't like the way the conversation was going. She wanted to know more about Luisa and the family, not talk about the *sistema*. This morning might be the only time she and Luisa would be alone.

"Tell me more about Diego; how is he doing in school?"

She made a face like she smelled something bad.

"Diego, my baby brother . . . He thinks he's so smart and tough. He's not. He doesn't like school, says it's a waste of time. He and Mamma argue all the time. Mamma picks on me, too," Luisa said, her words flooding out. "She doesn't like my clothes. Says I wear too much makeup. I use my phone all the time. She knows I smoke sometimes; she smells it in my hair."

Antonella had smelled it, too, as soon as Luisa had melted into her arms in the doorway. But she didn't smell smoke in the apartment. Possibly Luisa went onto the balcony, where Antonella could see a chair and table with an ashtray.

Luisa continued.

"I don't smoke that much, really, not like other kids. I don't smoke marijuana, even though my boyfriend wants me to. Mamma doesn't like my boyfriend, either."

"You have a boyfriend?"

She nodded.

"Luigi, he's eighteen. I like him, but sometimes he pushes me, wants me to do things that I don't want to do. I don't want to get pregnant and leave school. I see what happens when girls—some younger than me!—get in trouble and ruin their lives. I won't let that happen."

"That's wise, Luisa; you're much too young."

"I'm sixteen. I have my whole life ahead of me."

"Yes, you do. The next few years will be important: going to university, deciding what you want to study, making new friends, and eventually getting a job."

"You know what I really want to do, Zia? Go to music school!"

"Really?"

"Yes! Do you want to see my violin?" She pointed to a metal stand by the window and a violin resting on an open instrument case.

Luisa's cell phone buzzed.

"Oops, wait a minute, Zia. This is my friend; we have a violin lesson this afternoon." She clicked on a text message, replied without looking up, and then put the phone down. "We're meeting at her apartment before our lesson. Come, look at my violin. I was practicing when you knocked."

They got up from the sofa and went over to the music stand. "I was practicing boring scales. My teacher says scales are important, so I do them, but mostly I like to play concertos and sonatas."

"I played piano when I was your age," Antonella said. "I also didn't like to play scales."

"I tried piano, but it wasn't right for me, sitting on a bench, learning all the keys, and not playing all the right notes. My hands are small, see?" She held out her hands, nails painted bright red. "I couldn't reach some of the notes on the piano; it's so wide," Luisa said with a laugh. "So, I switched to the violin, which I can hold close, almost like a kitty. That's my real love."

Luisa's mood had changed, from grief and the stresses of a family undergoing bereavement to joy.

"Could you play something for me?"

"Really, you want to hear me play?" Luisa reached into the instrument case, lined in red velvet, and picked up her violin. She caressed the instrument, running her fingers along the smooth surface.

"I like the feel of a violin; it has a faint smell of old wood," she said. "I take good care of it, wiping it off with a cloth after I practice.

Sometimes, when I'm home alone, I open the case and just look at it. It's so beautiful, don't you think?"

"Yes, it is."

"During lessons, our teacher tells us about the master violinists—Paganini, Spohr, Kreutzer, Oistrakh. Do you know about Jascha Heifetz?"

"I do. He was a Russian violinist and performed all over the world. He was quite famous."

"At practice last week, our teacher played a CD of Heifetz performing a violin concerto. Toscanini was the conductor. Heifetz was a genius when he was a teenager. Imagine that! A teenager, just like me, performing concerts all over the world. How did he get to be so good when he was so young?"

"Heifetz was a prodigy. Do you know what a prodigy is?"

"I do, like a genius of sorts. I want to know how Heifetz got to be so good. He really was. Are geniuses born that way, or do they have good teachers?"

"Who knows?" Antonella said, enjoying the easy flow of the conversation. The mournful tension had dissipated.

"Can I show you what I'm learning?" Luisa touched the bow to the strings. "My teacher is helping me learn the *spiccato* stroke."

"What's that?"

Luisa bounced the bow off the strings, making quick notes. "*Spiccato* is when you tap the strings with the bow, not stroke it. It sounds easy, but it takes practice to get the right sound."

Luisa performed the stroke again, moving up strings to make higher notes.

"That's really good, Luisa. You're learning a technique. I'm impressed."

Luisa held her violin out to Antonella. "Here, hold it—my little kitty. She's so precious." Luisa was smiling, cheeks blushing with pride.

Antonella held the violin and gently touched its strings. One was like thin lead from a pencil, another like a dull knife, and the thinnest, almost as sharp as a razor blade. She ran her fingers over the wood base, cool to the touch.

"You're lucky to have such a beautiful instrument," she said, handing the violin back.

"Do you know the violin strings?"

"No, I don't."

"A violin has only four strings, G, D, A, and E, from lowest to highest. You touch the G string first, which makes the lowest notes. The E string is thinnest, the sharpest—you could cut your finger on it."

"I noticed," Antonella said, smiling.

Luisa beamed, cradling her instrument. "I love my violin—'my kitty,' I call it sometimes—but not in front of my teacher."

"Your teacher would understand. Maybe she had a pet name for her violin when she was your age."

"One of Papà's friends bought my kitty for me. It's from Cremona and expensive, I think. My teacher told me so."

"She would know. The best violins in the world are made in Cremona. That's where Stradivari made violins. Cremona also has a very nice violin museum."

"That's what my teacher said. She said I should go there and learn how violins are made."

"You should go there one day. You would learn a lot."

Luisa sighed. "I know, but Mamma says she's too busy to take me."

"Could you play something for me?" Antonella persisted.

Luisa made a faint grimace.

"Really, you want me to play for you?"

"Yes, I do."

Oh, I'm not very good, Zia. I practice every day, but I don't play well in front of people. I don't even like to play sometimes when Mamma's home. I'm afraid she'll criticize me, make me feel bad."

"I won't criticize you, Luisa. I'd just like to hear you play something."

"Well. Maybe . . . I guess." Luisa pulled out a cloth from the case and tucked it between her left shoulder and long white neck. She rested the violin on the cloth, picked up the bow, and stroked it across the strings. She reached up to tune a peg at the top of the strings.

"The D string was a little flat . . . I fixed it." She ran the bow across the strings.

"I play scales and *arpeggi* to warm up. I'll start with a simple G major scale." She stroked the bow across the strings; high- and low-pitched notes filled the apartment; then she bowed a chord, running up and down the scale. Luisa hummed along, her tones going higher to lower.

Luisa stopped playing the scale, plucked the strings with her index finger, making sharp, pinging sounds.

"This is *pizzicato*, plucking the strings with your fingers." She plucked other strings, making lower to higher sounds.

"I'm right-handed, as you can see. You can learn how to pluck with your left hand, but that's really hard. Paganini could do left-hand pizzicato and composed several concerti. His most famous was "Caprice No. 24," which is *sooo* beautiful. Rachmaninoff composed a rhapsody based on it. Have you ever heard it?"

"No, I haven't," Antonella said. "Your teacher is teaching you more than just how to play the violin. You're learning musical history."

"It's so interesting, don't you think? Let me play the G major scale and then a little concerto I'm learning." Luisa played the G major scale, up a few notes, and then descending. She stopped and turned pages on the music stand.

"Now I'm going to play one of my favorites, Felix Mendelssohn's 'Concerto for Violin and Orchestra in E Minor.'"

Luisa began the concerto, her dark eyes half closed as if she were in a dream, lost in her world of music. Beautiful, flowing passages from Mendelssohn's concerto filled the apartment with a rich, melodious sound, like streams of warm water.

Antonella held her breath, transfixed by what had happened in the last few minutes. This wasn't a teenager practicing scales, but a young, poised artist performing as if she were on a concert stage before an audience.

Luisa played the Mendelssohn concerto for several minutes, becoming more relaxed, bringing out beautiful passages that Antonella had heard professional musicians perform.

Antonella swelled with pride. Her sixteen-year-old niece was an aspiring musician, possibly taking a path to become a young artist with a career that could bring her joy, fulfillment, and a purpose. And a life far from the dangers of Napoli.

For the first time since she had arrived, Antonella was glad that she had come to Napoli.

CHAPTER FOUR

Antonella parked in the lot on Corso Duca d'Aosta beside the Pianura police station, a two-story stucco building with Italian and Euro flags drooping from flagpoles. A Polizia di Stato guard stood at the entrance in the shade, away from the intense sunlight, cradling an automatic weapon, his sunglasses shielding his eyes.

Antonella entered the station, reached into her purse for her DIGOS identification, and handed it through a slot in the bulletproof window to an attractive, dark-skinned woman about thirty-five years old whose hair was woven in long, thick braids.

"I have an appointment with Commissario Belmondo," Antonella said as the woman recorded Antonella's name and badge number into the station log book. She punched a button on the desk phone. After a brief exchange, she returned Antonella's identification.

"Someone will be with you shortly, Dottoressa Amoruso. Please have a seat," she gestured to plastic chairs, an ashtray stand, and a bench with *La Repubblica* and *La Gazzetta dello Sport* newspapers discarded by previous visitors.

Antonella sat farthest from the ashtray stand, which reeked of stale smoke and snuffed-out cigarettes. She took out her phone and texted Lucchini that she was at the police station to meet Commissario Belmondo. Next, she texted Carlo and Marianna telling them she had met Luisa at the apartment and would see Carmela and Diego that night at the Vesuvio Pizzeria.

A steel vault door opened, and a female officer greeted Antonella.

"Dottoressa Amoruso, follow me. Commissario Belmondo is expecting you." The officer had a stocky frame and muscular arms.

The escort led Antonella down a hallway to an elevator that they took to the second floor. No casual conversation, no eye contact, just the whir of the elevator. When they got out, the escort led her down a hallway lined with photos of police officers at official ceremonies receiving awards and commendations.

Antonella was two steps behind the escort and noticed she had a slight limp and favored her right leg. Her gait was like a marching soldier, arms to her sides, back stiff, head high. Had she injured a hip or leg in a police action? A training accident?

She opened a door with a plaque that read "Commissario Pasquale Belmondo" and gestured for Antonella to enter.

Across the room, Belmondo stood and came around his desk to greet her.

"Welcome back to Napoli, Dottoressa Amoruso," he said, shaking her hand and motioning to an empty chair in front of his desk. "How was your flight?"

"Routine. I left Linate at five, got to my hotel before eight. I'm staying at the International."

"How are things with DIGOS in Milano?"

"You know what happened last Friday at the EXPO opening," she said.

"Yes, of course, the riots, cars burning, and No Expo demonstrators. Quite a nasty bunch they were, spoiling the festivities on opening day. There are always troublemakers who want to ruin something we should all be proud of."

"So true," Antonella agreed. "When I got the call Monday to come to Napoli, I was in a security briefing at Expo about the demonstrators and rioting with the Carabinieri, Guardia di Finanza, Army, and DIA. It was frustrating for all of us, but at least the riot police on the streets were prepared. A dozen police were injured, none seriously, but still, an unfortunate way to kick off Expo. I hope that's the last of it."

Belmondo took his seat, leaned back in his chair, reading glasses perched on the bridge of his nose, a stack of documents on his desk, flags and certificates behind him.

"It will be a busy summer for DIGOS, no doubt. Do you have projections on how many people are expected to attend?"

"Fifteen, maybe twenty million. We have high-level security at the pavilions, and at airports, train stations, subways, and tourist sites."

"Yes, so I've read in the reports," he said.

"I witnessed increased enhanced security at Linate last night," she added. "Army guards at the entrance, in the concourse, and the gates. I was glad to see that."

"With the media attention, Expo will certainly be a target for terrorists."

"We'll be ready," Antonella said. "Morale is good. At the briefing yesterday, we learned that many police are volunteering for extra duty, weekends, and nights."

"I'm taking my family in August," he said. "We want to sample the foods from countries like Mexico, Cuba, and South America. My daughter is planning a trip to Japan next year. My son wants to go to Australia and New Zealand. Kids these days want to see the world, so different from when I was their age."

"You'll be impressed with the pavilions, very modern architecture, and state-of-the-art media. Japan's exhibit makes you feel you're in the country with tea shops, formal gardens, beautiful lanterns, and multi-media displays."

Belmondo cleared his throat.

"Nice to know, but you're not here to tell me about Expo. You'd like to know about our investigation into your brother's disappearance."

"Sir, I appreciate anything you can tell me," she said, respectfully dipping her head.

"I can brief you on the discovery of his remains, but I can't give you our official report," he said, placing a hand on a file on his desk, inching it toward Antonella.

"Salvo's remains were found about a kilometer from here between Pianura and Soccavo, near Via Vincenzo Padula, an area with abandoned buildings and empty lots. They were being developed until the 2008 financial crash. The developer went bankrupt, and the site was abandoned. A new developer bought it last year and started construction. When workers were clearing rubble, they found your brother's remains. I'm sorry."

"Thank you. What can you tell about my brother's murderers?"

"We suspect it was one or two members of the Leone family, rivals of your brother's clan. But we haven't been able to arrest them. We've questioned them, but they have alibis backed up by other family members. The Leone and Rocco clans have been feuding over who controls the areas between Pianura and Soccavo where they run drug operations, extortion, and low-level prostitution."

"I was raised in Soccavo," Antonella said, "just about the time it was being developed with the high-rise apartments you see now. It was a nice place to grow up."

"But now, Soccavo's overcrowded, has heavy traffic all day, and there's lots of crime. It's become a prime area for drug sales. That's why the Rocco and Leone clans were fighting over it. With the Camorra *sistema* now, it's all about drugs." Belmondo checked his watch, and then laid a hand on Salvo's file. "When was the last time you saw Salvo?"

"Four years ago, when I was here for the funeral of a friend's husband," she said. "It wasn't a pleasant meeting. Salvo was rude and insulted me, saying I was a disgrace to the family because I was police.

We quarreled; I told him he was the one who was the disgrace, a criminal. He said he was proud that the Rocco family had made him an 'honorable' man. That's ridiculous, of course; all that means is that the Roccos would take care of his family if he were ever jailed—or murdered."

"And they have. Carmela and the children receive financial support, at least the salary he was getting at the motorcycle shop where he worked."

"He was always into motorcycles," she said. "He stole a Vespa when he was fourteen and crashed it. Unfortunately, I was riding on the back, and we both ended up in the hospital. I didn't know he'd stolen it; otherwise, I never would have ridden with him. He was arrested in the hospital."

"Really? That's not in his police record," he said, nodding at the file on his desk. "Juvenile records are filed separately."

She waved a hand in a display of futility. "I don't talk about that incident much; it wasn't one of my best decisions to ride with him. After that, the tense relationship we had deteriorated further and never improved, unfortunately. Salvo became hostile to me, and I wouldn't see him for weeks. Our father was very strict with him, and Salvo rebelled against our family. I'm sorry about that. Maybe, if he and our father hadn't quarreled so much, things could have changed, and Salvo's attitude would have been less hostile." She sighed, looked down and then up at Belmondo. "But we can't change the past."

Belmondo nodded. "I'm sorry to hear that. Events like that, parents and children quarreling constantly, can have long-lasting consequences."

"They can. And did." She paused. "And so, we're here now. Talking about his murder."

Antonella felt a wave of sadness talking openly about her fractured relationship with Salvo, something she only did with her husband, boss, and sister. The pain of having a criminal as a family member was a personal and lifelong embarrassment.

It was quiet for a few moments. Belmondo sensed she was experiencing a painful moment. He cleared his throat. "Let me get back to Carmela and her relationship with the Roccos."

"Yes, please," she said, eager to move forward and learn about his murder.

"When he disappeared," Belmondo continued, "we learned that Carmela was promoted at the pizzeria where she had been a waitress. We learned on phone taps that she remodeled the apartment when she was given what would have been Salvo's payment for a drug operation. And someone bought the daughter an expensive violin."

"I saw it this morning at the apartment," Antonella said. "It's from Cremona. I'm sure it cost several thousand euros."

"The *sistema* keeps family loyalty with bribes, gifts, and social bonding. We know that Carmela and the children attend mass with Rocco families. I'm sure there are other social gatherings; clans like to keep families in distress close so they know they'll stay loyal."

"And from what I can tell," Antonella said, "Carmela was the emotional strength in the family. Salvo had a traumatic childhood, which I'm sure affected his marriage. His mother died when he was three years old. Our father married my mother, and Salvo lived with them until my sister and I were born. According to my father, Salvo was jealous, angry, and resentful of us. He did horrible things when we were just babies. So, my father sent him to live with an aunt and uncle in Scampia."

Belmondo looked down at Salvo's file again and checked his watch. "If you'll excuse me, the vice questore wants me to come to his office for a meeting about Salvo's funeral. If you don't mind, I'll leave you but will be back in about ten minutes."

Antonella was puzzled. They were going to discuss Salvo and the *sistema*, but suddenly he excuses himself? Then she began to suspect it was an unspoken signal to her. Police regulation dictated that official files weren't shared unless crimes crossed into another agency's jurisdiction. Belmondo was excusing himself and leaving Salvo's file on his desk. He didn't offer it to Antonella, which would violate regulations, but allowed her access without actually giving it to her.

"I'll wait here," she said.

"Fifteen minutes, maybe twenty," he said as if it were a coded message. Belmondo took off his reading glasses and set them on his desk, pushed back his chair, and left his office, closing the door with an audible click.

Antonella heard his footsteps down the hall and then a door open and close. She glanced around Belmondo's office to see if there were windows into other offices. Nothing, except a small window behind his desk with a view of a church steeple.

She checked her watch, twenty-two minutes after the hour. She reached for the file.

Salvo's name and his police identification number were printed on the front. She opened the file, which was divided by a series of dated tabs and contained official documents. The first pages were official police photos, profile and front, of Salvatore's first arrest in 2004 for selling drugs. Another, in 2007, for beating up a Leone clan member in a bar brawl. Again, in 2009, for extortion of a taxi company. The 2007 and 2009 photos looked nearly identical, except in 2007 he was wearing a black T-shirt, and in 2009, a white, wrinkled shirt with an open collar, revealing a tattoo on his neck. She studied Salvo's face, his eyes narrowed, a defiant stare, a week of stubble, lips pressed tight, corners of his mouth turned down. His lawyer got him released from the first two charges because of a lack of evidence. The extortion charge had been delayed, scheduled for trial, then delayed again.

The last tabs, the thickest sections of his file, documented his disappearance in 2013 and the discovery of his body. Statements by police officers who investigated his disappearance were documented, along with comments from Salvo's business partner at a motorcycle shop, Carmela's testimony of the last time she had seen him, and what neighbors in their apartment building said about him.

The next tab documented the discovery of the remains by workers at a construction site. Their statements were reported, along with those of the police who received the call, went to the site, and called for the forensic team.

After the statements, there were several crime-scene photos of investigators in white coats, plastic over boots, sifting dirt and rubble in a shallow pit, where other investigators stood over a corpse. Close-up photos showed the partial skeleton, later identified as Salvo, covered in dirt. Two bullet holes in the back of the skull, execution style. His hands tied behind his back with wire and wrapped around his body. No shoes; scratches on his feet and soles.

She flipped through more grisly crime-scene photos, sickened by how Salvatore was murdered, his body discarded like garbage into a pit. The coroner's report stated the exact date of Salvo's death could not be determined accurately due to decomposition.

Antonella closed the file and laid it back on the desk. She bowed her head, absorbing the shock of the grisly photos and the coroner's report. Images she could never erase. The most searing memory was of their last conversation, when she flew to Napoli for the funeral of a close friend's husband. She had called Salvo to tell him she was coming and wanted to see the family. He ignored her messages until the last afternoon, when he knew she was soon to leave.

He had left a message to meet for coffee at 1:30 p.m. at a café in Pianura. A difficult task, since she would have to race back to the airport for her 4 p.m. flight. He was waiting under an umbrella, smoking a cigarette, wearing fake designer sunglasses. Their embrace was quick, he mumbled something she couldn't understand, and they sat down.

"I hoped to see the children, Salvo," she said, a nervous edge to her voice. "How are they?"

"Fine. I don't want that, just me and you. That's it."

"Why?" she asked, her plea evident in the tone and force of her voice.

"No," he said shaking his head, lighting a cigarette with the butt of his last. "Maybe next time. When are you coming back?"

"I don't know," she pleaded. "My job is demanding; I work late, some weekends. I haven't had a vacation in a year."

"Yeah, too bad."

"That's why I called you and said I didn't know the next time I'd be here. I really want to see your family. It's been a long time." The emotion in Antonella's voice alarmed a couple at the next table, who turned to look at them.

He dismissed her plea with a shrug, took a draw on his cigarette. "Family?" he questioned. "Maybe by blood, nothing else. I don't want to talk about them. Tell me, why are you a cop?"

She knew they were headed down a blind alley. He wouldn't allow her to see his family, Talking about her career was erecting a wall between them. "It's my life, Salvo," she started. "I believe in justice. Without it, civilization would become a jungle."

He snickered. "Yeah, kinda like here. I like it; it's my life."

She wasn't sure what he meant. It sounded like a confession, a cynical confession. He stood up, crushed the cigarette in the ashtray, leaned down, and spoke quietly.

"We may not see each other again, Nelluccia," he said, using the pet name he called her when they were young. In another context, it could have been affectionate, but the way he snarled it, it was an insult. "We both carry guns. We might have to shoot someone so they don't shoot us first."

Antonella was stunned at his declaration. "What do you mean?"

"It could happen at any time," he said. Then he put on his sunglasses, turned, and walked away, leaving Antonella speechless.

It was the last words they shared. She could still see the intensity in his dark eyes and the searing tone of his voice. Their last meeting haunted her for a long time.

She checked her watch, thirty-four minutes past the hour. A few minutes later, she heard steps coming down the hallway. The door opened; Belmondo was back.

"Thank you for waiting," he said, returning to his desk. "The vice questore has made the decision that there can be a public funeral. We don't allow public funerals when *camorrista* bosses die or are murdered. But Salvo was not a boss, and the Rocco and Leone clans have been reconciling. We don't think there will be a disruption at the funeral. It's customary for rival families to attend funerals as a sign of respect, even if they were involved in the crime, so the Leone clan will be there—but so will we. We'll have plainclothes officers in the crowd and patrol cars blocking street traffic during the funeral procession."

"Those feuds never end."

"But sometimes they evolve into a truce. I've seen it. Changes happen in the *sistema*. Older leaders, men in their 50s and 60s, die, are murdered, sent to prison, or pushed aside by a generation of younger, more ambitious men who want to make changes in their criminal enterprises. That happened in the Rocco and Leone clans. After Salvo was reported missing, there was a shaky truce. They stopped feuding and divided up territories. Both clans distribute drugs but are getting away from prostitution and extortion. One big drug shipment can give them solvency for months. Comparatively, extortion of small businesses and running prostitution rings are not worth the time or petty returns."

Belmondo cleared his throat, looked at his watch. "Before you leave, I should tell you about Salvo's son, Diego."

Antonella wrinkled her brow. "What about Diego?"

"Well, unfortunately, he may already be involved with the Rocco family. He could be on his way to follow in his father's path."

"How is Diego involved?"

"He and other boys have bikes. They get tipped off when a drug shipment has arrived and is ready for sale. They bike to areas where drug addicts hang out, tell them where to go that night to get drugs. The pushers use an abandoned building or warehouse and sell drugs out of windows or in dark hallways. The boys on bikes hang out at intersections, watching for police cars. When one is driving toward the warehouse, the boys race through alleys to warn the pushers. By the time we get there, we find addicts passed out in the weeds or alleys. We find bodies as well; some haven't had a fix in a couple of days and overdose."

"My Soccavo neighborhood was poor, and there was always petty crime, but nothing like you're talking about."

"The drug shipments coming from Spain are the largest we've ever seen. They're smuggled on container ships, offloaded, and then gangs take them for analysis to test their potency. The clans get their allotment, maybe thirty kilos. They cut it with baking powder or flour until they have doses they can sell. When they're testing doses, they'll give it away free to addicts. They learn quickly if it's too powerful; we'll find bodies in ditches with needles still in their arms."

"Is Carmela involved in any criminal activities?"

He shook his head. "We don't think so. She hasn't been questioned or seen with any Rocco wives or girlfriends that we know are involved in selling drugs. The Rocco clan launders drug money through businesses like Vesuvio and meet in a back room. We planted a bug there a couple of years ago, but they ripped it out and we haven't been able to install a new one."

"I hope she doesn't join that life. While I'm here, I hope to talk to her about choosing a better life. Luisa plays the violin—that could be a path for her away from crime."

"I hope she listens to you. How long will you be in Napoli?"

"I leave Friday. I wanted to stay a day after the funeral to spend time with the family. I'm meeting Carmela tonight at Vesuvio. Is it safe for me to go? As soon as I walk in, they'll know I'm Salvo's half-sister and I'm with DIGOS."

He smiled, shook his head. "Don't worry, you'll be safe. They usually have a guard at the front door and won't let anyone in if they're suspicious. Carmela likely told everyone that you're coming. They won't mind; you're from DIGOS, not local police. If someone tries to approach you that they don't recognize, they could get roughed up and kicked outside."

"I'll have bodyguards at Vesuvio?" she said with a wry smile.

Belmondo chuckled. "Not a bodyguard—consider it 'family protection.' In the *sistema*, clans look out for each other. If someone crosses a family member, shows disrespect, they could get pushed into traffic or get a knife in the back. The *sistema* maintains a code of conduct based upon what they call 'respect.' Violate it, and one day you'll pay."

CHAPTER FIVE

VESUVIO

A tall, wiry man with a dragon tattoo snaking up his arm caught Antonella's attention as she approached Vesuvio Pizzeria. The tattoo was shocking, a long twisting reptilian tail with a scaly spine and a gaping mouth with shark-like teeth and flames shooting out of its nostrils. In its scaly fists, the dragon clutched a young woman in distress. Was this the guard that Belmondo said monitors the entrance so rival clan members can't enter?

Antonella stopped momentarily by the curb, a few feet from the entrance. She didn't notice a gang of teenage boys had been following her after she parked and were now behind her. In seconds they surrounded her; one boy jostled her from behind, another bumped her toward the curb, a third grabbed at her purse. She stumbled, caught her balance before falling into the traffic of honking cars and noisy motorcycles.

Napoli, early evening, a lone woman on a crowded sidewalk. The perfect target for a hasty grab and run.

The boys laughed and to passersby appeared to be simply pushing their way through pedestrians, but they had circled their target and were about to snatch Antonella's purse and push her into the street.

Antonella knew she was in danger and had to defend herself. She clutched her purse, stabbing her fingernails into the boy's hand who had grabbed the straps.

"Aah!" The boy grunted and called her a *puttana*.

Antonella couldn't see their faces but felt the boys pushing her closer to the curb. One on her left, another behind, a third gripping the purse straps. A hand wrapped around her waist, fumbling around her hip where her Beretta was holstered.

She jabbed left with one elbow, hitting one boy in the stomach. She wrenched back the boy's fingers from her purse until she heard a "pop" sound.

"Stronza!" the boy screamed, pulling his hand away.

Antonella lifted a foot and stabbed her heel backward. It hit a hard surface, not a cement sidewalk, more likely metatarsal bones.

She heard a "Uuuuh," and the hand around her hip pulled back.

Antonella was about to scream when a hand reached out and pulled her away from the boys.

"Hands off that woman!" the tattooed man swore, kicking one of the boys in the knee. The boy fell forward, dropping his grip on Antonella's purse, collapsing on the sidewalk screaming, holding his knee. The two other boys rushed around Antonella, picked up the boy on the sidewalk, and shuffled away from the tattooed man.

"Andate! Andate!" the tattooed man yelled. Two boys held the one with the injured knee by his arms. He was limping, favoring his right foot. The kicked boy turned around and swore at the tattooed man, "Go to hell, faggot!"

The tattooed man laughed, "Don't come back, children; I'll break bones next time!" He made a gun with his fingers. "I'll remember you!"

One of the boys made an obscene gesture and cursed, *"vaffancullo!"*

The tattooed man steadied Antonella on the sidewalk. Her right arm gripped her purse close to her side. Her heart was thumping so hard she felt as if it would burst through her chest.

"Careful, *signora*! You could have fallen into the street," he said calmly, a cigarette dangling from his lips.

"Th—thank you," Antonella stammered, regaining her balance. She blinked nervously and looked at people passing by, all unaware of what had just happened.

The tattooed man released his grip on her arm. "Let me help you. Are you going into Vesuvio?"

She looked up, her first close look at his face. Bright, shiny dark eyes, an anvil-square chin, long thin nose, and a hairline scar on his right cheek.

"Yes," she said, her voice shaky.

"Be careful walking alone in Pianura. Teenage thugs get rough around here at night. Let me get the door for you," he said as he opened it. "Enjoy your evening! Vesuvio makes the best pizza in Napoli."

"Thank you," she mumbled, eager to get off the street. She was grateful he had rescued her from a possible theft—or worse. But Antonella didn't want to see him again. Or talk to him. She hated tattoos and could never understand why people would willingly scar themselves for life with offensive designs or banal words.

She entered Vesuvio, her heart pounding as she recalled the attempted purse snatching seconds ago. She could still feel the boys circling her, a push, a shove, a grab for her purse, almost falling into traffic. It happened so fast, like most accidents.

The tattooed man had probably seen many purse snatchings and pickpockets. He seemed almost nonchalant, as if he rescued people every day. Then he politely greeted and opened the door for her. She'd been rescued by a man who seemed threatening at first sight but then became her savior.

The incident lasted only a few seconds, from safety to threatened theft, possibly injury, and then a dramatic rescue. It flashed through her mind. And again.

Antonella was safe inside Vesuvio but needed a few moments to recover. She had been in Napoli for twenty-four hours and was accustomed already to the gritty Pianura suburb: laundry hanging from apartment balconies, clusters of satellite dishes on rooftops, mountains of garbage bags spilling onto the streets and piled on filthy recycle bins. But she wasn't as cautious as she should have been.

Her heartbeat finally slowed. She took a deep breath. The clatter of dishes from the kitchen and the chatter of customers eating and drinking helped to restore her composure. She stood just inside the pizzeria; no one had seen her enter or noticed her momentary panic.

Antonella took another deep breath and scanned Vesuvio. She didn't want to appear as if she had just escaped thieves on the street. She felt safer now seeing chefs working in an open kitchen, waiters and waitresses delivering platters of pizzas, pasta, wine, and beer to customers at tables. Men sat on stools at the bar, some also tattooed, drinking Sambuca, watching a soccer match on a wall-mounted TV.

Antonella took a few steps into the pizzeria and caught the attention of a young waitress passing by with a tray of pizzas and beers.

"I'm looking for Carmela," Antonella said, raising her voice over the kitchen clatter.

"Yeah, are you Salvo's sister from Milano?"

"Yes."

"Gimme a minute, *signora*," the waitress said, rushing to deliver the tray to a table of men drinking beer under a neon sign. All had tattoos.

When she returned, the waitress said, "Follow me. We have a table reserved in the back." The waitress maneuvered between the tables, leading Antonella past the open kitchen to a semi-private room with two empty tables. The waitress snatched a *"riservato"* card off a table and stuffed it into her apron pocket. "You want a drink, maybe?"

"Please, Prosecco. And a plate of olives."

She nodded. "Got it. I'll tell Carmela you're here."

Antonella chose a chair against a brick wall with faded prints of old sailing ships in the Bay of Napoli, tourist posters of Capri, Vesuvio, Positano, and maps of Italian wine and pasta regions.

She began to relax and hung her purse on the back of a chair next to her. The room had a view of most of the pizzeria, the front door, the open kitchen, and the bar. The atmosphere was noisy with conversations and kitchen clatter. Chefs shuffled sizzling pans of fish, chicken, and pork simmering in wine or marinara sauces over flaming burners, slid them onto plates, sprinkled on cilantro, basil, cheeses, and spices, and then raised them to the counter for pickup.

Antonella spotted Carmela helping a young woman prepare salads, chopping arugula, radicchio, and tomatoes into metal bowls and sprinkling on olive oil, vinegar, and lemon juice.

She heard someone shout as the front door opened. The man with the dragon tattoo entered and was greeted with cheers as he made his way between tables, stopping to chat with customers until he reached the bar and ordered a drink. He was obviously well known at the pizzeria.

Tattooed Man picked up a glass of Sambuca, tossed it back, and asked for another. While he waited, he waved in the kitchen. Carmela waved back, wiped her hands on a towel, and went to the bar. They embraced, exchanged cheek kisses, and started talking and laughing.

Who was Tattooed Man? More than just a sentry. A friend of Carmela's? Had Carmela told him she was coming and he was waiting for her to arrive? Or was it just a coincidence?

The waitress returned with a glass of bubbly Prosecco, a ceramic sleeve tray with green and black Sicilian olives, and a basket of sliced bread.

"Carmela knows you're here," the waitress said. "Diego is working in the back; he'll be out, too."

Antonella sipped her Prosecco, not taking her eyes off Carmela and Tattooed Man talking at the bar like old friends. Carmela looked in Antonella's direction and their eyes met. She said something to the man, pointing to Antonella. He nodded and gave a quick hand wave. Carmela said something else and then returned to the kitchen.

Antonella pondered, *What was that exchange about? Had she asked him to come over and meet her? Who was he?*

She took another sip of Prosecco, enjoying the cold, bubbly wine sliding down her throat. She picked up the menu comprising two pages of pizzas, two of pasta and salads, and a dessert page with *gelati*, cookies, and cakes.

She put the menu down and looked into the kitchen. In front of the pizza oven, she recognized Diego, wearing a chef's hat and apron. He wasn't washing dishes but sprinkling pepperoni, salami, mozzarella, basil, mushrooms, and onions onto slabs of pizza dough. When Diego finished dressing the pizzas, he said something to a chef, who scooped the pizzas onto a wood platter and slid them into a wood-burning oven. He was making pizzas? Luisa had just said he emptied the garbage and swept floors.

A shadow in the doorway blocked Antonella's view.

"*Ciao*, Antonella."

It was Carmela, her apron spotted with splotches of olive oil and tomato sauce. Antonella rose, they embraced, exchanged cheek kisses.

"I'm so glad you're here Antonella; thank you for coming," Carmela said. "I couldn't meet you this morning, two of our staff are on holiday. I asked for the week off, you know, the least you would expect. But no, all I got was tomorrow and the rest of the week. Can you believe that? I've worked here for more than eight years and can't even get the week off for my husband's funeral!"

"I'm sorry . . . I had a nice talk with Luisa this morning."

"Yes, she told me. She'll be here soon. Let's sit down; I've been on my feet all day."

"Did I see Diego making pizza?"

Carmela laughed. "Yes, the little guy wants to be a chef."

"He looks serious, very absorbed in rolling dough, sprinkling salami and mozzarella on it."

"He is dedicated—when he's making pizzas. But most of the time, he's not a happy kid. He's picked up some of Salvo's bad habits; he's moody, likes to argue, says bad things."

It had been only two years since she had seen Carmela, but she appeared to have aged five. Faint wrinkle lines radiated from Carmela's eyes, a fold of flesh around her neck. She had gained weight; her hips looked like she had gloves in her pockets.

Carmela sighed. "A waitress is bringing me a Prosecco. I need to relax; I'm tired," she said, her voice weary. "It's been a long day. I can't work as long as when I was twenty—and before I had kids."

A good beginning, Antonella thought. *She wants to talk woman to woman, not like adversaries.* In the past, Carmela had been aloof, not opening up about her family. Antonella suspected that Salvo didn't want his wife to be close to her sister-in-law.

"Age is catching up with us," Antonella answered. "I have trouble sleeping through the night."

"Me, too! And when I wake up, I'm still tired. It's frustrating."

"We're getting older, Carmela; time marches on."

"Yes, it is . . . too fast for me," she sighed.

Antonella reached across the table, put her hand on Carmela's. "I'm sorry about Salvo. He was . . ."

Carmela looked like she might cry, but no tears came, only another sigh.

"Yes, we all knew this day would come. The children are devastated, of course, but I accepted the inevitable a long time ago. The children kept hoping he'd walk through the door and say he's been on a long trip. But they knew . . . they just didn't want to admit it."

The waitress returned with a glass of Prosecco for Carmela, who took a long sip and said, "I still cry at night sometimes . . . but that will stop one day. I hope soon."

"It's natural to cry, Carmela," Antonella said. "I cried last night." A small lie; she had a moment of sadness when she went to bed but then fell asleep without a tear.

In the brief moments they had been together, Antonella felt that Carmela wanted to open up to her, but on her own terms. There was so much to talk about: the trauma of Salvo's horrible murder, the loss of her husband, and the uncertainty in her life. But she would let Carmela take her time.

"I'm sure you want to know some of the . . . circumstances I didn't go into when I called your office," Carmela said.

"Take your time, Carmela. I'm here to listen and help."

Carmela exhaled, releasing the stress of the last few days. "Well, let me start with Wednesday, the day the police called, saying they wanted me to come to their office. They'd recovered Salvo's body and needed me to identify his clothes, watch, and ring. I didn't want to see his body—or what was left of it. Just bones, I'm sure." She shuddered. "I'd never . . . ever want to . . ." She couldn't finish.

"I met Commissario Belmondo this afternoon," Antonella said. "They have confirmation from Salvo's dental records."

Carmela nodded, strands of loose hair falling in front of her eyes. She brushed them away. "Let's not spoil dinner tonight talking about this. You and I can talk about Sal later."

"That's fine; we'll have time."

"I want to tell you about the next couple days before Diego and Luisa come. Tomorrow we are meeting the priest about the funeral. Then a private dinner with friends from Vesuvio and Sal's motorcycle shop. Then the funeral Thursday morning at eleven."

"Carmela, I'd like to help pay for the funeral."

"No, no," she said, shaking her head. The strands of hair fell again, and she brushed them away. "It's taken care of."

"Really?"

"Sal's friends paid for everything—the casket, flowers, burial, and a donation to the church."

Antonella was not surprised; the *sistema* supported families when a father, son, or brother got in trouble or was killed. Paying for funerals was part of the arrangement for the "honored society." Antonella was furious; Salvo died because he was an "honored member" of the Rocco clan. Funerals were just a business expense for them. But how does a family replace a father and husband? She could never be a part of any such arrangement. They were criminals. She wanted nothing to do with that kind of enterprise.

"Which mortuary is making the arrangements?"

"De Cataldo on Via Venezia."

Antonella assumed the mortuary provided discounts for the "honored society." After all, they were steady, reliable customers of the mortuary. And they paid their bills on time.

"I'd like to help."

"Not necessary. Would you like another Prosecco?" she asked, nodding at Antonella's half-full glass, changing the subject.

"No, I'm fine. I'll wait until the children join us."

"I'm around food all day, and the last thing I want is to eat what I've been preparing. I'll just have a salad."

Antonella wanted to know about Tattooed Man.

"Carmela, who was that man you were talking to at the bar?" Antonella hoped she didn't sound too assertive.

"Who? Oh, that was—"

"*Ciao*, Carmela, I'm here," a woman interrupted.

Carmela looked up. "Oh, I'm glad you're here. Antonella, this is Maria, my replacement. Excuse me, I'll be right back. I need to talk to her for a moment."

The two women left the room and went into the kitchen. Antonella didn't learn who the man was. She couldn't ask again; it would arouse Carmela's curiosity. She'd have to drop it.

Antonella twirled the Prosecco glass in her fingers, taking small sips. Dragon Tattoo Man was still at the bar, drinking red wine now, nibbling cheese and crackers, talking with the men watching the soccer game. Someone scored a goal; the bar erupted in cheers, high fives. Another round of drinks for all.

Antonella glanced over as the front door opened and saw Luisa enter and pass through the restaurant, waving toward the kitchen. Luisa rushed into the private room and greeted Antonella.

"*Buona ser*a, Zia Antonella! I'm so happy you're here. Don't you like Vesuvio?"

"I do. I'm starving smelling all the aromas coming from the kitchen. I saw Diego making pizzas."

Luisa laughed and sat down next to Antonella. "Silly boy, he loves to make pizzas. When he comes home after work, he brags that he's a pizza chef. I told him he'll become fat like a pig if he makes and eats pizza every day."

"How was your violin lesson?"

"Good! I like my lessons," Luisa said, her voice bubbly. "We listened to a Mozart concerto and practiced parts of it. It was hard, lots of complicated chords and very fast. I've never been able to play it."

"Don't give up. Practice, learn your scales. Your teacher will help you. You'll be surprised how quickly you can learn difficult passages."

"You think so? My teacher says that."

"She's inspiring you. One day, you may perform at a recital."

Luisa rolled her eyes. "Oh, I wish! I could if I practiced like my teacher wants me to."

"You will." Antonella reached over and squeezed Luisa's hand. She could feel affection growing between them, warm and natural. In past visits to Salvo's family, there were few occasions of affection, only tension and anxiety. Antonella had never felt close to any of them because of Salvo's hostility. In just a few hours, Antonella could feel emotional bonds beginning with Luisa and Carmela.

"I'll bet you're hungry?" she asked Luisa.

"Starved! I didn't have time for lunch. And I'm thirsty."

"I've ordered water; it will be here soon."

Luisa took her cell phone out of a back pocket, flipped through texts, and put the phone back.

"Zia Antonella, I'm so glad you came. We needed to see you. You're so different from Mamma's friends. They work here or live near our apartment. They're nice, but they live like us, boring, you know? But you live in Milano and have a career. You dress like a professional woman.

I love your clothes, your shoes, your purse. You look fashionable, like a model, almost!"

Antonella laughed, reached over to pat Luisa's arm. "Not really, models are all young and skinny. That's not me."

"Oh, you know what I mean. You look so good in your clothes."

"I'd buy you some clothes if I knew what you liked."

"Really? My favorite store is Dolce & Gabbana! They have clothes for teenagers."

"I'll do it. I want to help your family any way I can."

"Really?"

"What else do you need?"

Luisa shrugged, reached up with a napkin to pat the sweat on her brow. "I don't know . . . not money. Just, you know, come see us more."

"Would you like to come to Milano? It's been years since you visited with your mother. You were only five or six and stayed only one night."

"I love your apartment; it's incredible. I couldn't believe my *zia* lived in a building with marble floors, modern furniture, a balcony with a view of the canals."

"The Navigli is a very popular place with restaurants, art galleries, and neat shops. Next time you visit, we'll go shopping there."

Luisa sighed. "Oh, Zia, I'd really like to. Milano is more beautiful than Napoli! That's what I think, anyway."

They heard a scuffling, looked up. Diego stood in the archway, wearing an apron, his wavy black hair tucked under a chef's cap. Diego had grown taller in two years, no longer a gawky adolescent. He resembled his father, high forehead, wide, dark eyes, thin lips. Although a young teenager, Diego was handsome in an adolescent way. It wouldn't be long until he became irresistible to girls.

"Hello, Diego," Antonella said, coming around the table to exchange cheek kisses. Diego pushed back, resisting her embrace.

"Mamma said you were here."

"You've grown taller, Diego. You're a nice-looking young man."

He ignored her comment, took off his cap, and ran his fingers through his long hair.

"Come sit by me," she said, taking his arm. "It's been two years since I saw you. You look like your father."

"He's dead, you know. That's why you're here."

"I'm so sorry, Diego, very sorry. He was a good father."

"Yeah, I guess," he said, sitting down next to Antonella, across from Luisa. He slumped in his chair, looked across at his sister, and greeted her with a finger wave.

"You've got tomato sauce on your apron. Gross," Luisa said.

"Forget it," he said. "I'm working, not fooling around."

"I was at my violin lesson, not fooling around!" she protested.

He shrugged, looked away.

Antonella didn't like the bickering. She didn't want the evening to be petty squabbling between teenagers, even if they were her nephew and niece.

"Children, I came to Napoli to be with you and your mother," Antonella said. "We're a family. We help each other during difficult times."

Diego smirked, partially closing one eye, looking over at Luisa and then back at Antonella. "You don't live here! You're from Milano," he sneered.

"Diego!" Luisa blurted out. "Don't be rude! She's our *zia*."

Antonella maintained her composure. She was disappointed but not surprised by his comment. Diego was behaving like his father, pushing people away with insults. Was this his normal behavior, or was he testing Antonella to see how she would respond? He'd likely picked up critical things Salvo had said about Antonella.

Before he died, Antonella's father said that Salvo was a good boy when he was young. He went to church, obeyed his parents, and played well with other children. But his personality changed after his mother died. It was a turning point in his life. Antonella's father said Salvo became morose, withdrawn, and difficult to deal with. He picked fights with other children and argued with teachers and neighbors. After their father married Antonella's mother and started a new family, Salvo became angry and often cried. He did poorly in elementary school and had few friends. It became obvious that he didn't want to share his father with his new step-mother, and eventually with Antonella and Marianna when they were born.

Diego shrugged. "It's the truth! Zia doesn't live here. She says we're family, but families live in the same town, not far away. Milano is, you know, like Switzerland. It's all rich people They're arrogant and despise us in the south. All northern Italians care about is money."

"Stop it!" Luisa shouted.

Antonella put a hand on her arm. "That's all right. I understand."

Antonella looked at Diego with a placid smile, not expressing the anger or disappointment she felt because it would only make him more defiant.

When she interrogated a suspect, Antonella's face was a mask. She did not reveal emotion, just a neutral expression. She asked questions, hinting she knew more than she actually did, and then listened without interrupting. When a suspect was evasive or offered a benign comment, Antonella waited and then asked another question. She played a game in which her tactic would get the suspect to reveal information, drop by drop. Each answer gave Antonella a thread to her next question. The interrogation tactic was slow and frustrating, but with patience and persistence, suspects often revealed important information, unraveled word by word, sentence by sentence.

From training, Antonella knew that police rarely learned anything by being antagonistic or using threats. Her tactic was to ignore insults or threats and to just keep asking questions and listening.

"Diego, Milano is my home," she said deliberately, looking into his dark eyes. "Yours and Luisa's is Napoli. I was born in Napoli. I went to school here, like your father. When I was eighteen, I left for university in Roma. But Napoli will always be my hometown."

He nodded slowly, emotion drained from his face, absorbed in Antonella's soft tone and words. Antonella let her words sink in. When she continued, her voice was soothing.

"Diego, your father and I had the same father. We—your sister," she nodded to Luisa and then to him, "and you and your mother and me are one family."

"Are you still *polizia*?"

"Yes, I am."

"Why?"

"Police uphold the law."

He frowned, wrinkles creasing his forehead. "Police are corrupt, just like judges and lawyers. They're all criminals."

"Not all of them, just those who make bad decisions. They pay for their mistakes. Some are tried in court and go to jail for years. The police I work with are honest. And hardworking."

"Nah," he snarled. "Maybe in Milano, but not here."

"There are good police in Napoli, also. Italia needs a strong police force."

"Maybe, but they don't. They're all corrupt," he sneered.

"Is that what you hear? It's not true, Diego—take my word for it."

He shrugged and glanced at Luisa, avoiding Antonella.

"Are those things that you hear about at school? Do your friends tell you police are not honest?"

He ran his fingers through his hair, squirmed in his chair, tapped a foot on the floor.

"Sometimes, yeah. I hear stuff like that."

She put a hand on his arm. "You're upset about your father, Diego. He was my half-brother. We had the same father. That makes us family."

"Yeah, OK—if you say so."

"Let's take time to be nice to each other," she continued. "I want to help you."

He shook his head. "How? You're here for Papà's funeral, and then you'll go home. Isn't that right?"

"Stop it!" Carmela said, walking into the room. "What are you say-ing to your *zia*?" She had taken off her apron, applied lipstick, mascara, combed her hair, and put on a blue blouse, white slacks, and strappy shoes. Not a cook or waitress anymore, but a middle-aged mother.

"Mamma, Diego isn't being nice to Zia Antonella," Luisa said.

"What did you say, Diego? Show respect; Antonella is your *zia*. And a police officer! She doesn't have to listen to rude boys like you."

Carmela sat down between Luisa and Diego, not taking her eyes off him, his head lowered. "Look at me!" She slapped the table. "Tell Zia you're sorry for acting like a brat. Now!"

He pushed back in his chair, bobbed his head side to side. "All right, all right, I'm sorry, Zia Antonella," he mumbled.

Antonella squeezed his arm. "You're my nephew, Diego. I care about you, your sister, and your mother."

The waitress came in with a basket of sliced bread, bottles of natural and carbonated water. They paused, leaned back in their chairs, poured water into glasses and took sips. Diego grabbed a slice of bread from the basket and stuffed it into his mouth. A silent truce.

"Are you ready to order?" the waitress asked, looking around the table.

"Sure, I want a pizza," Diego said. Antonella and Carmela ordered salads, and Luisa asked for linguine with clams.

After the waitress left, Carmela said, "No more trouble, Diego. Antonella is our guest. Be nice to her."

Diego grabbed another slice of bread and looked at Antonella. "Can I see your badge?"

Antonella paused. Police regulation said officers could show their badges only as identification or during an investigation. She reached for her purse, took out her leather-bound identification and showed it to him. He reached for it, but she held it firmly. He narrowed his eyes to read.

"*Divisione Investigazioni Generali e Operazioni Speciali*. What does that mean?"

"DIGOS investigates people suspected of being terrorists."

"Oh, you mean immigrants?"

"Not always—it depends."

"Do you arrest them?"

"Sometimes."

"Have you ever killed someone?"

She paused. "I'd rather not say."

"So, you did."

Antonella didn't respond.

"Were you scared?"

Antonella took her time responding. "Police don't have time to be scared in dangerous situations; things happen very fast."

"Do you have a gun?"

"Stop it!" Carmela said. "Now!"

"Can I see it?" He persisted.

Antonella shook her head.

"You're a pest," Carmela said. "Zia Antonella has a very important job."

"How do you get a police job?" he said, ignoring his mother.

"The standards are very high for good reason," Antonella said. "They don't take just anybody. Police recruit men and women with university degrees or sometimes law degrees like I have. You need good references and no police records. There are many tests, interviews, and rigorous physical training. Thousands apply, but only a few are accepted."

He shook his head. "They wouldn't take me," he said sullenly.

"You're too young. You have to be at least twenty years old."

"I've been in trouble with the police."

"She doesn't need to hear about this," Carmela interrupted. "It was a year ago."

He ignored his mother. "They asked me questions in the back of a police car. People were selling drugs. Some of my friends were involved."

"Why were you questioned?"

He shot a glance at his mother; her jaw clenched.

"The police had a video of me riding my bicycle when police cars showed up and arrested people."

The waitress came in with their dinner, setting plates and bowls in front of each. Diego sliced a piece of his pizza, picked it up, and stuffed it into his mouth. Carmela, Luisa, and Antonella waited until everyone had been served and then started eating in silence, creating an uneasy tension with the fragrant aromas of pasta, tomato sauce, salami, and parmigiana at their table. Antonella didn't want the tense mood to linger and spoil their meal.

"Diego, you might be in a similar situation again. Napoli has clans who teach boys to carry out criminal acts. Soon the boys are known by the police, and they often end up in jail."

He finished his first piece of pizza, cut another, and took several bites before he answered. "I know about that. I'm not afraid."

"You're young, growing up fast. Decisions you make today or tomorrow could affect your entire life."

"Yeah, I know that," he said flippantly.

"Do you want to be questioned by the police again?"

He shook his head. "No. Never!"

Antonella said, "Will you promise your mother it will never happen again?"

He looked at Carmela. "Yeah, I will, Mamma." Then with a smile on his face, he turned to Antonella and asked, "You know what I really want to do, Zia Antonella?"

"What's that?"

"I want to make pizzas!"

Luisa chuckled, "You already do that, silly."

"Tell me why you want to make pizzas," Antonella said.

Diego's smile turned into a grin. "Because I love to! When I started working at Vesuvio, I emptied garbage, cleaned tables, and washed dishes. I hated those jobs, but when I finished, I helped the chefs making pizzas: sprinkling flour around the table, rolling the dough, stretching it, sprinkling sauce, mozzarella, and salami. One day I asked Carlo—he's the main pizza chef—how he learned to make pizzas. He said his mamma taught him when he was a boy."

"You never told me that," Carmela said.

"Why should I? You're always mad at me," he snapped back.

"But—"

He continued. "I asked Carlo if he would teach me. One afternoon when it wasn't busy, he showed me how to make a pizza. All the way from rolling the dough ball and flattening it into a circle, to adding the salami, mozzarella, tomato sauce or whatever the customer ordered. Then we just slide it in the oven for two to three minutes. You don't need much time; the oven is more than 900 degrees. When it comes out, you use a rocking knife, you know, like a sword almost, to slice it," he said, making a rocking motion up and down with his flattened hand sideways, rotating in a circle over his plate.

"You do that at home!" Luisa said, making the rocking motion with her own hand. They were all smiling, enjoying Diego's story.

"Three slices in the dough . . . six pieces . . . you've got a pizza," he continued, making the slicing motion again, more exaggerated.

"One afternoon, I asked Carlo if I could make a pizza while he watched me. A waiter called out an order for a pizza. Carlo told me, 'This is your first pizza order, Diego. Can you make it?' 'Of course!' I said, and I did. I rolled a fresh ball of dough, stretched it, sprinkled cheese, tomato sauce, basil, and olives, with Carlo watching me like a teacher. I put the pizza in the oven, checked the clock. After two minutes, I took it out, sliced it—" he made the slicing motion again and made everyone laugh, "—put it on a plate and gave it to the waiter."

They all laughed. Diego was pleased with himself, changing the mood with his funny story. He looked happy for the first time that evening, grinning, his dark eyes sparkling.

"That's a wonderful story, Diego. I like to see you happy like this," Carmela said, a smile also lighting up her face.

"Mamma, I'm not done! When the waiter served my pizza to the customer, he pointed into the kitchen, called me 'little pizza man, Vesuvio's newest pizza chef.'"

"You're so funny, you make me laugh, silly boy!" Luisa said, grinning at her brother, who was clearly enjoying the attention.

Diego raised his hand. "Wait! I'm still not finished. The customer ate a slice, rolled his eyes, and waved at me."

More laughter—this time even Carmela burst out.

Diego continued, "Guess what happened next?"

"Tell us!" Luisa demanded.

Diego was beaming like a child opening a Christmas present. He held up his hands as if he were about to make an important announcement. "Guess what? The customer gave the waiter five euros—he told him to give it to me as a tip."

He reached into his pocket, took out a crumpled five-euro note, and dropped it on the table. The colorful note looked like it had been balled up, flecked with pizza dough, discarded in a drawer, and forgotten like a piece of trash.

"Mamma, my first tip!" His grin was wide, showing bright white teeth.

The room exploded in laughter, especially Diego, who raised his arms in triumph like a soccer player who had just scored a goal. "I want more tips! I want more tips!"

The laughter continued with smiles all around the table as Diego picked up the crumpled note and tossed it into the air. When it landed on his pizza, he picked it up, kissed it, then placed it in front of Carmela's plate.

"What do you think, Mamma? Can I be a pizza chef?"

Carmela grinned. "Diego, I'd love it if you became a chef—maybe a famous one who owned a restaurant."

"Or had a TV show!"

"I would have given you ten euros if I'd been your first customer," Antonella said. "Maybe you could make a pizza for me one day."

"I will! Can I make it in Milano?"

Antonella looked across the table at Carmela. She shrugged, eyebrows raised.

"I don't know; maybe. If Zia Antonella wants you to."

Antonella smiled. "Maybe this summer you could come to Milano and make me a pizza."

"Really? Yes, I will!"

CHAPTER SIX

WEDNESDAY

On Wednesday morning, Antonella parked across the street from the De Cataldo funeral home. A sign in the window read: "Comforting the Family in Your Hour of Need." Below the sign was a color print of a bouquet of lilies.

The façade was brown stucco with white trim and a red tile roof. The sidewalk in front of the funeral home was clear of litter and dried leaves, apparently hosed down that morning, a faint stain of evaporated water at the curb.

Antonella pushed open the door and entered an air-conditioned reception area; the air was cool, with a faint metallic odor. A man in his forties was reading a newspaper at a mahogany desk and looked up when she entered. He quickly took off his reading glasses, folded the newspaper, and came out from behind the desk. He approached Antonella, his hands folded in a prayer-like pose as if he were a priest. He was clean-shaven and wore a black suit, white shirt, and shoes so small that his pant legs covered all but the tips of his toes. His brown hair was bushy like a puppy's and combed in a style that made it look like a bad wig.

"*Buongiorno, signora,* my name is Ernesto. Welcome to De Cataldo's," he said. They shook hands, and then he resumed his prayer pose. "How may I help you?"

"My name is Antonella Amoruso. My brother was Salvatore. I'd like to talk to you about his funeral tomorrow."

Ernesto bowed respectfully. "I'm sorry for your loss, *signora,*" he said, his voice low and pious like in a confessional. "Please accept my condolences. Would you like to come over here where we can talk?" He gestured with an outstretched arm like a maître d' leading a customer to a reserved dinner table.

Antonella followed Ernesto across a dark navy carpet toward his desk with three sofa chairs in front of it. She took a seat, and he hurried behind his desk, snatching his *Gazzetta dello Sport* newspaper and stuffing it into a drawer.

"How may I help you, Signora Amoruso?"

"I would like to pay for Salvatore's funeral service."

Ernesto's eyes widened as if Antonella had uttered a curse word. "But that's not necessary, *signora.* The funeral has been arranged."

"So I was told," she said, not wanting to admit that Carmela had informed her last night. "Will you tell me who paid for your services?"

Ernesto blinked several times. He cleared his throat and then said, "All arrangements have been paid for by friends of his family."

"Who, precisely?"

Ernesto flinched. "I'm sorry, *signora,* that is a private matter . . . all has been arranged, as I said."

"You won't tell me who paid for his funeral?" she persisted.

He raised his hands like a priest about to say a prayer. "Funeral arrangements are private matters, arranged between the family and De Cataldo's. I'm sure you understand; families who use our services want the arrangements to be private."

"Did his wife, Carmela, pay for the funeral?" Antonella asked, knowing full well Carmela hadn't.

Ernesto squirmed in his chair, uncomfortable with explaining the delicate protocol of who actually pays for funerals. Someone dies, the family meets with representatives of a mortuary, money changes hands, the business deal is finalized. No one outside the family or mortuary discusses the details; the matter is too personal and gauche for idle gossip.

"Well . . . I don't have permission to discuss—"

"Carmela did not pay for the funeral. Someone else did."

He nodded deferentially. "That's right."

"I don't want to have it 'arranged,'" she said firmly. "*I* will pay for his casket. You can refund the people who arranged it."

"But—I don't understand," he pleaded.

Antonella held up her hand. "Stop, please—did you hear what I said? Refund the cost to whoever paid you. As I said, I will pay for my brother's casket and your services." Antonella refused to allow *camorristi* to pay for her brother's burial and service.

"But—"

She rose from her chair.

"Sir, if you don't have the authority to fulfill my request, let me talk to your supervisor."

Ernesto's face twitched like he'd chipped a tooth. He squirmed and then said, "Would you excuse me, *signora?*"

He stood, turned around, and walked to a purple curtain behind his desk, disappearing behind the curtain, the thick folds rippling and closing without a sound. What or who was behind the curtain?

Antonella heard a muffled voice. Ernesto's, speaking rapidly, his voice rising, but she couldn't hear his words. Another voice behind the curtain, a woman's. More mumbling from Ernesto, and then the woman asking questions, Ernesto answering. A long question from the woman, a brief two- or three-word response from Ernesto.

The woman's voice was muted, speaking slowly, seeming to calm Ernesto. A moment of silence. Another exchange: she asked a question, and Ernesto answered.

The muffled conversation behind the curtain lasted for more than two minutes. The curtain parted, and an older woman with gray hair tied in a bun emerged. She wore a black dress with a white collar and a strand of pearls around her neck. She was thin, almost gaunt, with long arms, a bracelet on one wrist, a wedding band on her left hand. She bore the presence of a former nun. Or funeral home owner, which she probably was.

"Signora Amoruso," she said respectfully, her face void of emotion. "Please, could you wait a moment? I will make inquiries about your request. This may take a few minutes." She smiled formally and disappeared behind the curtain, which ruffled and closed again silently.

Antonella attempted to picture the drama behind the curtain. Ernesto likely wringing his hands, his face sagging, at the mercy of two strong-willed women who would dictate terms he would have to obey. He could be the kind of man who often found himself in that position because he had never quite been able to exert authority in personal or professional situations. He would defer to figures of power, at home and in the workplace. If he was married, his wife was probably a tyrant. She commanded; he obeyed. No debate.

It was quiet for a few moments, then Antonella heard a monologue, the woman talking. She guessed the woman was on the phone. She talked for almost a minute and then paused, listening to the response. The conversation continued and then ended with the typical Italian blizzard of "*Ciao . . . ciao . . . grazie . . . grazie . . . ciao . . . ciao.*"

Antonella checked her watch, noting the time. A phone rang behind the curtain. The woman answered, uttering unintelligible words, but Antonella heard anxiety in the woman's voice.

Antonella turned an ear toward the curtain, straining to hear the phone conversation. She could make out single words at the beginning of a sentence, but then it turned into a muffled rush of a one-sided conversation.

Two phone conversations. With whom? Would there be a third or fourth call? Antonella waited. An exchange between Ernesto and the woman, low and incoherent, lasted another minute.

The phone rang again. The woman answered, listening without responding. The phone conversation ended with the woman saying, "Yes . . . certainly. Goodbye." Another muffled conversation between the woman and Ernesto; she did most of the talking.

Antonella looked at her watch. It had been almost ten minutes since Ernesto had disappeared behind the curtain.

Then it reopened. Ernesto appeared, his face ashen—as if he had received a guilty verdict from a judge. He sat down and, with a handkerchief, wiped his damp brow.

"Signora, would you like to look through our catalog?" He asked, his voice breaking. He reached for a leather-bound book on his desk.

She shook her head. "I don't want to look at pictures. Do you have models I could see?"

He looked surprised like someone had poked him. "Why of course, but we usually don't show them to families unless they request to see them. Most are satisfied to choose from our catalog."

"Do you have a display of caskets I could see?" she persisted.

He pushed back from his desk and returned to the curtain, opened it, and said, "Signora Amoruso would like to visit the viewing room."

"Very well, take her," the woman said from behind the curtain.

Ernesto closed the curtain and hurried around his desk, taking quick steps as if he wanted to get this duty over with so he could return to his sports newspaper. "Would you follow me, please, *signora?*"

He led Antonella toward the rear of the reception area, pushing back another curtain into a room that resembled a modest chapel. Two gold candle holders with unlit candles, a vase of white roses, and a gold cross lay on a small altar. The glow of sunlight through white lace curtains illuminated a painting of Jesus behind the altar, crucified, eyes closed, a crown of thorns on his head.

Ernesto gestured to a hallway left of the sanctuary. She followed him, passing an open door to an office with a desk, lamp, a bookcase with leather-bound books that looked to be religious texts.

They proceeded down the hallway. On the right, an array of prints hung on the wall depicting early twentieth-century popes, who resembled medieval kings seated on thrones, holding miters. They each wore a peaked hat adorned with jewels, ornamental vestments draped over scarlet and gold robes, a large gold chain, and a cross over their chests.

On the opposite wall, Antonella looked at prints of more recent popes, Pope Pius XI and XII, John XXIII, Paul VI, John Paul I, John Paul II, Benedict XVI, and Francis. Their vestments were modest, white robes and skullcaps, small gold crosses, and they were seated by a table with an open Bible. For a moment, Antonella imagined she was not in a mortuary but entering a private office in the Vatican.

Ernesto waited for Antonella at the end of the hallway, looking as beatific as the popes, but without a white cap or gold cross. He gestured with the maître d' sweep of his arm into a carpeted room with open caskets on raised platforms. The room also looked like a chapel, with small statues of the Virgin Mary, paintings of Christ as an infant, with his disciples at the Last Supper, and crucified on the cross. A small chandelier lit up the room as bright as a surgical ward.

Antonella had a moment of unease, viewing caskets in glossy walnut and mahogany, glistening like new sports cars. Their lids were open for mourners to view where the deceased would lie.

Ernesto gestured at a large, navy-blue casket. "This is the model purchased for your brother's service."

She stepped on the platform to inspect the interior. A white linen sheet with lacy borders covered a mattress. A red satin pillow without a wrinkle or crease rested at one end. On the velvet-lined lid above the pillow was a hand-painted print of the Virgin Mary holding baby Jesus on a cloud, halos over their heads.

Antonella's fingers gripped the edge of the casket, repulsed by the gaudiness. Salvo's casket would be closed, draped with flowers. Who would care what the inside of his casket looked like? Not Carmela or the children.

She inspected two more open caskets that brought to mind painful memories of funerals she had attended in Milano that year. She felt nauseous, recalling those services, the reminders of mortality, the familiar, somber rituals of white-robed priests reciting prayers, altar boys bearing crosses, the smell of incense, marble altars adorned with gold crosses, a sculpture of the crucified Christ, head sagging, bloody gash in his side, feet nailed to the cross.

Antonella embraced life, people she loved, art and culture that celebrated beauty and dignity that would never die. She was anxious to leave but determined to get what she had come to De Cataldo's for.

She turned to Ernesto, whose hands were still folded in a prayer pose.

"These caskets are . . . too much. Do you have something simpler? My brother was not a saint; he was a common man with a family. I don't think they would have chosen one of these caskets," she said as she stepped off the platform.

Ernesto was puzzled. This was his job, displaying caskets to grieving families. Rarely did they take more than five minutes to choose one and depart.

"*Signora*, most families choose one of these you see here," he stammered, gesturing to the models.

"These caskets look like they're from a Borgia funeral."

Ernesto winced like his toothache had returned and looked like he was about to cry.

"I prefer something more modest."

Ernesto took a deep breath, leaned back on his heels, and clenched his hands into fists.

"Show me a simple casket, please," she continued. "Salvo's casket should be as simple as he was."

Ernesto squirmed, clenched fists pressed against his thighs. "Well . . . if you would like—"

"Yes, I would. Show me, please."

They exited the display room. Ernesto hurried past the papal portraits, through the chapel, into the reception area. Antonella followed leisurely, satisfied that Ernesto respected her authority. He was just a mortuary attendant who likely used his deferential manner to put mourners at ease and peddle the expensive tools of his trade. But not today. Not with her. He would remember their encounter and likely share his experience with the bossy, gray-haired woman behind the curtain. And later that evening, with his wife, if he had one, who would likely smile to herself, knowing that once again a strong female had overpowered him, like tipping a turtle onto its back.

Ernesto sat at his desk, reached into a drawer, and pulled out a catalog. Antonella took her time before she sat down. He flipped pages, found what he was looking for, and turned it around to show to Antonella without looking up at her.

Antonella saw Ernesto's shiny bald spot, almost perfectly round, the size of a saucer. She hadn't noticed it before. He had combed his hair on the front, the sides, and in back to hide his bald dome.

He looked up after she had not spoken since she sat down. She knew she didn't have to rush; she would get what she wanted. Ernesto noticed her smiling, and then she looked down at the catalog. She leaned forward to look at the page displaying plain caskets in olive wood with faint trim on the borders. Most likely for families with modest means and little cash.

"I'll take this one," she said, pointing to a simple black casket.

Ernesto exhaled, sensing the anxiety of accommodating Antonella was about over. "An excellent choice."

She took her purse, opened her wallet. "How much? I'll pay in cash."

Ernesto flinched again, uncomfortable with Antonella's calm composure and confidence. "Well . . . yes, of course." He opened his desk drawer and took out a metal box with cash and coins in trays.

"How much?"

"Fifteen hundred euros, which includes three hundred euros for our . . . services."

She leafed through her wallet, extracted fifteen crisp one hundred-euro bills, and placed them next to the cash box.

Ernesto grabbed the bills and filed them into the appropriate trays. He pulled out a receipt book from his desk drawer, scribbled the date, the amount paid, and signed it. He ripped it out and handed it to Antonella.

He held his breath, hopeful that she would be leaving soon. He got up from his desk, retreated behind the curtain, mumbled something that probably meant Antonella had paid for a casket. A mumble from the woman, and he was back at his desk.

Antonella folded the receipt, slipped it into her wallet and put it into her purse. "Thank you." A polite smile, like one might flash to a waiter.

Ernesto pushed back his chair and reached over his desk to shake Antonella's hand. A limp, quick shake, his fingers cool and damp like a sponge.

"Thank you, *signora*," he said, his voice cracking. "It was an honor to serve you. Please express my condolences to your family."

CHAPTER SEVEN

S alvo's motorcycle shop, Motomania, had two doors, with one leading into a showroom displaying Italian motorcycles. Next to it was a repair shop with an oil-stained cement floor and metal cabinets containing tools and machine parts. When Antonella parked across from the shop, she saw two men in the repair shop hunched over dismantled motorcycles, hammering and drilling with electric tools.

Antonella crossed the street, maneuvering around a row of parked motorcycles at the curb. Antonella hated motorcycles. She knew they were dangerous, remembering her injuries when she was flung from Salvo's Vespa into a parked car. Since her accident, she had witnessed bloody, maimed bodies at crash scenes around Milano. Too many motorcycle riders were inexperienced, intoxicated by the power of the machine, unprepared for the dangers of hurtling down the Autostrada, and unable to react to debris on the road or a car that moved into their lane, or negotiate a curve at high speed.

A friend who worked at the hospital had told her that almost every day ambulances delivered injured motorcycle riders requiring multiple surgeries to repair broken limbs. The worst were those with brain injuries who would become burdens to their families and medical personnel.

A mechanic looked up when he saw Antonella. He stopped hammering and looked puzzled by the thought of a well-dressed professional woman entering the showroom. He watched her and then resumed working.

Antonella walked into the showroom, passing shiny red and black Ducati and Aprilia machines propped on kickstands. They looked aerodynamic, with side panels and fuel tanks designed like an airplane's fuselage.

A man and a teenage boy, possibly a father and son, were inspecting a red Ducati with a salesman. The boy was sitting on the Ducati, feet on pedals, looking in a sideview mirror, running a hand over the fuel tank like he was stroking a dog's belly.

But it wasn't the father and son who captured Antonella's attention. It was the salesman—the tattooed sentry from Vesuvio, kneeling, pointing at the coiled metal tube and chain connected to the rear tire. His long-sleeved shirt all but covered the tattoo; only the tip of the dragon's tail on his wrist peeked out from under his cuff.

The man rose, walked around the Ducati, describing the features of the bike.

". . . the Ohlins suspension system is the best in the world. In regards to—" He stopped talking abruptly when he saw Antonella. He blinked, his eyes widened, and a look of surprise crossed his face.

The father and son turned around and saw Antonella. She didn't acknowledge them; she looked only at the salesman, who had recovered from the shock of seeing her.

"Excuse me, please," he said to the father and son. "I'll be right back." He walked around the Ducati and approached Antonella near the entrance. "You're Salvo's sister," he said, more of a question than a statement. "The boys who tried to rob you in front of Vesuvio—I stopped them, remember?"

"Yes, thank you. Do you work here?"

"Yes," he said, smiling. This is my business."

"Salvo worked here, is that right?"

"Yes, we were partners."

"That's why I'm here."

It took a moment for him to comprehend. "I see . . ." he said, wanting to be respectful but knowing she was a police officer. Was she here to talk about her brother, or could there be another reason?

"Could you excuse me?" he apologized. "I'm alone and have customers. Do you mind waiting?"

"Not at all."

"Would you like a caffè or water?" He pointed to a counter with an espresso machine and small refrigerator alongside posters of motorcycles.

"I'll wait. Take your time."

"My name is Francesco, by the way." He raised his hand as if to shake hers, then dropped it to his side.

He returned to the customers, the boy still on the Ducati, smoothing his hand over the red cowling. "As I was saying," he continued, "the dry clutch sound which reverberates . . ."

Antonella walked over to the counter and retrieved a bottle of water from the refrigerator. She sat on a stool looking around the showroom at the gaudy motorcycle helmets, heavy gloves, pants, and black jackets displayed along the back wall. To her, they looked vaguely militaristic or like props from science fiction movies, appealing to men with superhero fantasies. But in reality, their function was to protect fragile bodies from collisions with trees, walls, vehicles, and asphalt.

One wall was covered with metallic decals of Italian motorcycle manufacturers: Garelli, Ducati, Fantic, Italjet, Laverda, MV Agusta, Aprilia, Cagiva, Borile, Beta, Benelli. In the corner, a vintage black-and-red Ducati was mounted on a platform as if it were a museum display.

A widescreen TV was tuned to a channel with the sound muted, showing motorcycles zooming around the Monza race track, riders leaning low around steep curves, their handlebars and gloved fists inches from the asphalt track.

Antonella sipped her water and overheard the salesman—Francesco—as his customers prepared to leave the shop.

"Next week, I'll take you both for a test ride," he said. He followed them outside, and the boy got on the back of a motorcycle parked at the curb. His father shook hands with Francesco, flung a leg over the seat, started the motorcycle, and sped off down the street.

Francesco returned to the showroom and came over to Antonella.

"I'm free now. Have you been in a motorcycle shop before, *signora?*" he asked.

"No, this is my first time," she said. "I wanted to see where Salvo worked."

He gestured to the motorcycles in the showroom. "This is it. Do you want me to show you around, to see what we do here?"

"Not really. You sell and repair motorcycles. I want to talk about Salvo. I knew he worked in a motorcycle shop but didn't know he was an owner."

"We were partners. We opened Motomania four years ago."

She nodded, waiting to hear more.

Francesco said, "Let's go into the office. We can talk better there. We don't get many customers until after they leave work."

He led Antonella behind the coffee counter into a semi-dark, cramped office with a desk cluttered with corporate brochures, manuals, motorcycle magazines, and paperwork. A motorcycle hubcap next to a desktop computer had been converted into an ashtray filled with butts and ashes.

"Have a seat, please," he said, removing magazines from a chair. He went behind the desk and dropped files and papers onto the floor. "What would you like to know about Salvo?"

"How did you know him?"

Francesco smiled. "Salvo and I were boyhood friends from the time we were six years old, after my family moved to Scampia from Caserta. We walked to school, played soccer, hung out with other boys on the street. When we got a little older, I think when I was about ten, I started helping my family in our fruit and vegetable market. About the same time, Salvo got interested in cars and motorcycles. He'd watch men working on their cars and motorcycles and tell me he couldn't wait until he was older and could ride motorcycles." He sat back in his chair and smiled at the memories.

"But you know, people in Scampia don't have a lot of money. You can't afford to take your cars to repair shops, so you learn how to repair them yourself. When we were about twelve years old, we started hanging around motorcycle repair shops. We wanted Vespas but, of course, didn't have money, and our parents were poor."

"Did you know he stole one when he was fourteen and wrecked it?"

He smiled. "Yes, of course. You were riding with him and ended up in the hospital, isn't that right? He bragged about it; it got him in trouble with the police."

"It did—he stole it. For three weeks I was in the hospital with broken ribs and a mild concussion. I haven't been on a motorcycle since. Did you know he had two younger sisters in Soccavo?"

"Of course, he talked about you after he'd come back from a visit."

"Did you ever have a motorcycle accident?"

He nodded. "More than one," he said. "That's how I got this." He touched the scar on his cheek. "I'm more careful now. I have a family."

"How did you and Salvo become partners?"

"When we were twenty, Salvo was working in a small motorcycle shop when the owner died. He persuaded the wife to hire me since I had apprenticed at another shop. We worked hard, and a year later we bought the shop from his wife. We made a little money, the business grew. After a while, we sold that shop and bought a larger one. I managed the business, sold motorcycles, and worked with customers. Salvo was a good mechanic; he could diagnose what was wrong with a machine, repair it, and make the customer happy. Our service shop always made money and kept us going when sales were slow. You sell a motorcycle, you make a little money. But you make more money when the customer needs repairs, tune-ups, and new parts. That keeps the business going," he said, gesturing to the door into the repair shop.

"Was Salvo a good partner?"

Francesco pondered his answer for a moment and then said, "More or less, he was. Not ideal by any means, but we stayed together. We've done well with this shop and location. Cars pass by every day on their way to Via Montagna Spaccata. Word gets around, customers from Napoli come because they hear about our good service."

"What will you do now that Salvo's dead?"

He frowned, shook his head. "It's a problem. I've been running the shop by myself for the last two years with a little extra help. I need a business partner, not just an extra employee or two. Someone who comes in early, stays late, and does things without having to be told. Salvo was that way."

She nodded, learning something about Salvo she didn't know. He took his business interests seriously, not just because he wanted to be around motorcycles all day.

Francesco continued. "After Salvo . . . disappeared . . . I had to hire other mechanics. But none of them are as hard-working as Salvo was.

"Before that, we had been talking about maybe buying another shop in Napoli. We could get the money, but I gave up that idea when Salvo . . . disappeared."

He sighed, looked into the repair shop and then back at Antonella. He looked sad, remembering Salvo and their partnership, now just a memory. "But life goes on," he said. "I work long hours and cut my salary; otherwise, I would lose this." He waved a hand around the office in a gesture of futility.

A movement in the showroom caught Francesco's attention. A young man had walked into the shop. "Excuse me, someone just came in," he said as he left the office.

Antonella got up from the chair and looked down at his desk. Two framed pictures stood by the computer. One was of Salvo, Carmela, and the children when Luisa looked about ten years old. In the other,

Francesco held a baby, one arm around an attractive woman who held the hand of a little girl about four years old with long, curly hair like her mother. Francesco was married with a family? He was *camorrista*, likely running a business with funding from illegal drug sales. Didn't he ever fear that his fate might be the same as Salvo's—leaving a widow with two very young children to raise by herself?

Antonella walked around the office, looking at magazines, posters, sales brochures, and an open box of motorcycle gloves on the floor. *How boring,* she thought, *a life built around ear-piercing machines that belched noxious fumes and caused serious bodily injuries.* She glanced into the showroom; Francesco was patting a young man's back as he departed.

Antonella returned to her chair as Francesco came into the office. "Just a friend," he said. "I asked him to come back later. What else did you want to know about your brother?"

"Did Salvo ever talk about me?"

"Yes, about you and your sister . . . I can't remember her name."

"Marianna."

"Ah, yes," he said raising his hands, palms facing each other, then touching. "He didn't say much, just that he had two little sisters, said you were spoiled, didn't like to do things he did."

"Like steal Vespas."

Francesco laughed. "Yes, but he said many times he didn't fit in with the family. He wanted brothers he could play soccer with, not sisters."

"That's true, but there's more than that. He was also very jealous because our father married another woman after his mother died. He was only three years old."

"I did know that, but he didn't talk about her much when we were young, just that he wished his father had wanted to raise him, not send him to his mother's family."

Antonella nodded, a bit surprised that Salvo would confess as much to another boy.

"Salvo was a lonely little boy," Francesco said. "I felt sorry for him sometimes; I was raised by my mother and father, not an aunt."

"It wasn't a good situation, but my father couldn't have him stay at the house with two young girls he resented. He was mean to us sometimes. There were months when we didn't see him. Our father wouldn't talk about him because Salvo was angry with him, especially when he started getting into trouble, fights in school, hanging out with rough boys."

Francesco nodded but remained silent.

Antonella continued, "Did he talk about me or Marianna later on, after you two started your business?"

"He did."

"What did he say?"

"He didn't say much about your sister; she was a teacher or something. But you were a cop. DIGOS, is that right?"

"Yes."

"He respected what you did . . . but he was also critical of you."

"Do you know why?"

Francesco pondered a moment before he answered. "In so many words, you left Napoli, deserted your family . . . that's what he said."

"Not true," she said, her voice sharp. "I didn't desert my family. I went to university in Roma and studied law. I came home often to see my parents. I called Salvo and asked if I could see his family. He wouldn't give me a direct answer, said he'd call later but never did. Eventually, I quit calling him."

He shrugged, shook his head. "I'm sorry, I don't know the details, but he was jealous. You made a life away from Napoli. You moved to Milano and married someone rich. He was bitter about people with money; it really pissed him off. He'd see a politician or banker on TV in a money scandal. He'd go crazy and swear at them, calling them 'scum' or something worse. Much worse."

"He certainly had a temper," she said with a nod. "I heard him go into rages about things, often trivial. He just couldn't stop himself."

"Yes . . . yes, it was one of the downsides of being his partner, listening to his rages."

Antonella changed the subject. She knew about Salvo's temperament but wanted to learn more about the Salvo she hadn't experienced.

"What kind of father and husband was he?"

Francesco smiled. "Salvo loved his family. He bragged about Luisa and Diego, said they would grow up and be successful. He brought Diego to the shop often when he was younger, showed him how motorcycles are built and repaired and took him for rides. Did you know Salvo raced motorcycles?"

"He did?"

"Yes, he was pretty good a few years ago. He raced at Monza once but didn't qualify for the finals." Antonella perked up; Monza was a suburb of Milano. Salvo had traveled there but didn't contact her. Why not?

Francesco got up from the desk, went to a shelf with photos and small trophies. He brought two photos to the desk and handed them to Antonella. "Here's Salvo and Diego after he'd won a race."

Diego, about eight years old, was beaming at his father, who was wearing a Ducati logo shirt and cap, holding a trophy. Their smiles almost matched, happy son, proud father.

He handed her another photo, Diego ten or eleven, standing next to Salvo, almost reaching to his father's shoulder. Holding a smaller trophy.

"That was the last race Salvo won. He continued racing, but the competition was getting younger, some fearless teenagers who had quicker reactions. Salvo was a skillful driver, but he took risks, passing on curves, gunning too fast on stretches. In his last race, he skidded, flew off the bike, cracked his knee, and broke an elbow."

"I didn't know that."

"He was embarrassed. And angry with himself, of course. When he came back to work, he needed crutches and his arm was in a sling so he couldn't work much, just tell the other mechanics what to do. That made him angry; I had to tell him to go home and rest. He cursed at me, but I made him leave. A couple of days later, he apologized. But I didn't like how moody he could be. Sometimes for days. He was even cruel to Diego when he came to the shop. I hated to see that. Diego looked up to his father but was also afraid of him."

"Fathers and sons don't always get along, especially during adolescence and the teenage years." She looked at the photos on the desk. "You have a family?"

Francesco beamed, glancing at the photo. "Yes, two little girls, Carla and Maria. My wife works in a nursery school."

She paused, weighing whether she should say what had been on her mind since seeing the photo.

"Don't you worry that what happened to Salvo could happen to you? Your wife become a widow, like Carmela, but with two very young children to raise?"

Francesco balked. He clenched his jaw, lips pressed together. When he answered, his words were clipped. "I . . . I don't want to talk about that. I won't let that happen. I'm not like your brother—"

"What do you mean?"

"I'm more cautious. I don't make foolish mistakes or get angry and say things I shouldn't. That was one of the things I warned him about, but he wouldn't listen."

"Do you know who killed him?"

It was as if a gunshot had gone off in the room. Francesco held his breath, eyes widening. The last few minutes they had been talking about Salvo's behavior. But Antonella, an acknowledged police officer, had asked a question with ramifications far beyond what they had been discussing. Pianura detectives had asked him the same question many times. His answer was always the same.

He stared coldly at Antonella. "No, I don't," the same answer he had given the detectives.

"I don't believe you," she said sharply.

They stared at each other across the table, neither one talking. The silence in the room made the tension grow as their eyes locked, their expressions frozen in confrontation.

Francesco blinked first. "I don't want to talk about this."

"I do," she countered.

"Are you here as a police officer?"

"No. I'm a sister wanting to know who killed my brother."

He shook his head. "I'm sorry . . . I can't help you. Talk to the police." He turned away, looking into the repair shop. When he turned back, Antonella saw grief on his face.

"Do you have anything else to say about Salvo?" she asked, sensing that their conversation had come to an end.

He shook his head.

"Then I'll leave," Antonella said, taking her purse off the chair beside her and setting it on her lap.

"Not yet," he said. He stood, went around, and closed the doors to the repair shop. "I don't know if I should say this—"

"Tell me," Antonella insisted. "I want to know."

"Only if you don't share with Carmela."

She nodded. "Of course, I keep confidences all the time."

"I think you want to help Carmela's family. I'm worried about them, especially Diego and Luisa."

"Why?"

He took a deep breath. "I've known Diego since he was born. Before I had children, he was like my own son. I watched him grow up. Now, he's vulnerable without Salvo. Every son needs a father to help him make the right decisions."

"I want to help but don't know what I can do. I came to Napoli for more than just Salvo's funeral."

Francesco nodded. "Yes, I thought so. Maybe you can help."

"I will if I know the situation better."

He continued nodding. "Something happened here a few days before Salvo disappeared. It involved Diego."

Antonella was shocked. "Diego? Tell me."

Francesco looked at Antonella without answering. She wasn't a mind reader but had plenty of experience questioning witnesses, suspects, or criminals holding back important information. Francesco was none of those. But if she was persistent or confrontational, he would resist and say nothing. She waited a minute, looking at Francesco without blinking, recognizing a flicker of something like empathy. He wanted to confide—she could read that on his face.

"Tell me, Francesco. You need to . . . for Diego's sake," she said in a gentle voice.

He took a deep breath. "Yes, you should know . . . like you say, for Diego's sake." He cleared his throat and then continued. "Salvo came to work; he wasn't feeling well but was our only mechanic that day. I wanted to send him home, but two important customers came in for major repairs and wanted to get their motorcycles back in a few hours. They were putting them on a yacht and sailing to Sardegna that night. Salvo was having problems with one of the bikes. He was frustrated, yelling that he wasn't going to get the job finished. Diego came in after school and went in to see Salvo. I was in this office; I could hear them. I don't know how it started, but Salvo started yelling at Diego. They shouted back and forth. I heard a tool get thrown against a metal cabinet and Salvo cursing at Diego. Diego screamed and ran out of the shop. He was crying. He got on his bike and went home."

Antonella visualized a frightened Diego running from his angry father, a memory that likely still haunted him.

"About a week later . . ." Francesco continued, "Salvo disappeared. The police came to talk to me. I didn't have any information to help them; I just said that he had been sick and missed work. But I didn't say anything about Diego."

Antonella nodded, suspecting he wasn't finished. Francesco shook his head, sadness on his face.

"Diego hasn't been to the shop since. The argument with his father was just too painful for him. I wish he'd come back, . . . but I under-stand. I might have done the same if it was me."

Antonella felt sad, compassionate toward Diego and the memory of the shouting match with his father he surely held on to. A crushing emotional burden. Did Diego think he was partially responsible? Was that why he was rude to her in Vesuvio? He was defensive, afraid of being hurt by someone else, and traumatized by the memory of his father arguing with him days before he disappeared and was murdered.

The stale air in the office was stifling. Antonella needed to leave, get in her car and turn on the air conditioning. Francesco could see the sadness in Antonella's expression.

"I'm sorry if I upset you; I didn't mean to. Diego is on my mind every morning when I walk in here."

Antonella held up a hand. "Thank you for telling me. Yes, I am worried about Diego and the family. One reason I'm here is to determine if there's a way I can help them."

"I hope you can. I respect you and . . . what you've done with your life."

Antonella got up and left the office, walking through the showroom to the door. A wall of muggy heat smothered her as she waited to cross the street. A motorcycle slowed, passed in front of her, and parked in front of the shop.

She got in her rental car, started it, and turned on the air conditioning. In the rearview mirror, she saw Francesco standing in the doorway, arms crossed. He raised a hand and waved toward her car.

Antonella drove away and resisted the impulse to look back.

CHAPTER EIGHT

After meeting Francesco, Antonella returned to her hotel room, kicked off her shoes, and sat on the bed. She checked her text messages from Carlo and Giorgio.

Giorgio was returning from Roma that afternoon and going to the office. Carlo apologized again for not joining her in Napoli and said he would call that night, which would be early morning in Australia. She responded that she was having dinner with Rosanna, a former class-mate at parochial school, who had been at their wedding. Rosanna was almost the only friend she could count on seeing when visiting Napoli. Rosanna had answered Antonella's text Monday afternoon and said she could meet Wednesday evening for dinner.

After Antonella freshened up and changed into a dress, she walked onto the balcony before she left for dinner. The sun was descending in the west, still fiery, shimmering off the vast blue waters of the Bay and the offshore islands. Vesuvio maintained its dominant presence in the south, a curl of smoke rising from the caldera, menacing but silent. She smiled, remembering her youthful memory that the volcano looked like two kittens under a green blanket.

Antonella enjoyed the tranquility of her hotel room away from the Napoli traffic and islands of garbage containers overflowing with plastic bags, bottles, and trash she had seen that day. She had fond childhood memories of Napoli, but the city seemed too noisy, dirty, and—rude. Was it just her, or did its residents feel the same?

The attempted purse-snatching incident in front of Vesuvio the previous night still frightened her. The shock of youthful thugs surrounding her, one grabbing her purse, another nudging her towards the curb and possibly pushing her into traffic if the purse snatching was successful put a knot in her stomach. She was relieved she acted quickly, digging her nails into the purse snatcher's hand and stabbing her heel into the foot of the thug behind her.

She could still feel Francesco's hand reaching out to rescue her from the thieves, followed by curses and obscene gestures from her attackers. It took only seconds to pass from safety to danger to being rescued. What if Francesco had not been there? Could she have fought them off, or would she have become a victim of a robbery—or worse? It had happened twenty-four hours ago, but the memory replayed in her mind like a nightmare. But it had happened. A fragment of the boy's skin had lodged under her fingernail. A smear of a dirty handprint stained her pantsuit. The memory of the curses and obscenities lingered.

But it was over. She was safe in the hotel now and looking forward to dinner with Rosanna. She glanced down at the hotel patio, guests lathered in sunscreen floating on plastic rafts in the pool, wearing hats and sunglasses against the bright rays of the evening sun. Children splashed in the shallow end, scooting down a slide. Guests drank cocktails and fruit juice under umbrellas, keeping waiters and waitresses busy taking orders and delivering trays of chilled bottles and light meals.

It had been only forty-eight hours since Antonella had arrived in Napoli, but it seemed like a week. She missed Milano and her colleagues at the Questura. She would be home in just two more days, but the next two days would be intensely emotional: Salvo's funeral tomorrow, the wake in the evening, and a few hours with Carmela and her family Friday morning. She needed to make the most of her remaining time with the family. A return trip to Napoli any time soon wouldn't be possible with the demands of Expo almost immediately upon her return, lasting until the end of October. In those six months, the fate of Carmela, Luisa, and Diego would likely be settled without her involvement.

At 7 p.m., she met Rosanna at La Cantinella in the historic city center near the Egg Castle. Rosanna was a striking brunette; she was wearing a blue linen pantsuit, a multi-colored silk blouse, and a scarf with bold sweeps of blue swirls. Over her shoulder, she carried a blue, soft suede Ferragamo bag.

"Welcome back to Napoli," Rosanna said as they hugged and exchanged cheek kisses. "It's been what, two years, I think? When you texted me, I couldn't wait to see you again."

"Much too long, I agree. We have a lot to talk about tonight," Antonella said as they took their seats in a secluded booth among the bamboo decor and hanging paper-globe lanterns. A waiter in a starched white shirt and black bow tie handed them menus and asked if they'd like to order drinks. They ordered mineral water and a bottle of Falanghina wine.

"I'm sorry about Salvo, Antonella. Please share my condolences with the family. I can't imagine what it has been like for them to learn what happened. Dreadful."

"Two years of not knowing," Antonella said. "Two years of agony. I'm seeing the emotional damage of all of them, anger, frustration . . . despair. It breaks my heart."

Rosanna shook her head. "I'm sure it does. Thank God you could come and be with them. How does a family cope when a father isn't there anymore? And murdered. What a tragedy."

"Yes, and some families don't cope at all," Antonella said. "The family bonds unravel, and unless they get help to deal with the grief, some family members never recover."

Rosanna nodded. "They need you; I'm sure you know that. You're strong and courageous."

"Thank you," Antonella answered quietly, feeling uncomfortable with Rosanna's praise. She didn't want to talk about herself, only the family. "I'm reaching out to them; the kids are growing up fast, and Carmela is struggling with what to do with her life."

"I'm sure you are offering her encouragement and hope."

The waiter delivered wine and water, poured a sample for each. They nodded; he filled their glasses, bowed and left.

They raised glasses, toasted "cin cin," and sipped their wine.

They looked around as more guests arrived at the restaurant, all elegantly dressed, the women well coifed, most of the men in designer suits. Antonella felt relaxed for the first time since she had arrived. And being with Rosanna was a pleasant reminder of happy times when they were younger.

"It's been more than two years, Rosanna. I want to catch up with your busy life," Antonella said, avoiding a direct reference to the death of Rosanna's husband, Gennaro, from a heart attack. He was ten years older than Rosanna and had been an executive with Tirrenia shipping, which ran ferries between Capri, Napoli, and Tunisia. Antonella had gone to Gennaro's funeral, but she and Rosanna had little time to talk other than offering condolences.

"We will, but first, tell me everything about what you've been doing," Rosanna replied. "You have such an exciting life, a senior police official in Milano, one of my favorite cities in Italia."

Antonella laughed. "Hey, we have only one night, but I want to know how *you've* been. How are things at the bank? You're a vice president, aren't you?"

"Yes, promoted last year. I was lucky to get hired by a friend of Gennaro's after he passed. You know, I didn't work when we were married. Gennaro loved to travel and took me to South Africa, China, Japan, Mexico, and the US several times. He didn't want me to work so we could take off anytime. 'I want to be free as a bird,' he used to say.

But after he died, I would have gone crazy without a career. I meet so many interesting people at the bank, mostly because I can loan them money!" She said with a throaty laugh.

"Congratulations! Having a good career is such a joy. It gives you purpose. And if you're lucky, you meet fascinating people."

"So true. And I have news: I bought an apartment in Posillipo," Rosanna said, her eyes shining.

"Posillipo, one of my favorite places in Napoli!" Antonella said. "I haven't been there in ages but have fond memories when we were young and had romantic experiences there."

"Oh, yes, many, many," she said with a smile, then sighed. "But I'm still single," she said, holding up her hand to show no ring on her finger.

"There are contenders, I'm sure. You're beautiful, full of life."

Rosanna waved her hand in a noncommittal fashion. "One or two . . . well, one, actually. But he's a baby, only thirty-six years old! I feel like I'm robbing the cradle. He's from a nice family. His older sister has two children; an older brother has four children. I see the families often for holidays and birthday parties . . . But enough about me; my life is boring compared to yours," Rosanna said. "Tell me about DIGOS. You're one of the top agents, aren't you?"

Antonella shrugged. "Deputy to the capo, Giorgio Lucchini. We've worked together for five years; we get along well and have a great team of agents working for us."

"From what I've read, you've broken big cases: the TAV bombing, the kidnappers of the American woman, and the Muslim terrorists at La Scala. Congratulations."

"It's always a team effort. We have some of the best police in Italia."

"And you're one of them," she said.

Antonella scoffed. "Please, I take credit for training them; that's my most important job. When they're assigned to us, we have a demanding training program, matching experienced agents with new agents and putting them on the street, so to speak. They learn fast or they're shipped out."

"Exciting work; I'm sure you enjoy it."

"I do. But I didn't come here to talk about my job . . . how boring. Tell me about your young man. What's his name?"

"Roberto."

"What does he do?"

"He has a good job: he manages a famous, old hotel that used to be a brothel. They're full almost every night with guests from international tour groups—French, German, British, and American."

"Do you think you have a future?"

She sighed. "Oh, I don't know. After Gennaro died, I wasn't interested in having a serious relationship. But last year, I met Roberto at a party. We went to dinner a couple of times, nothing serious. He had recently broken up with a girlfriend and was looking for female companionship. It was all friendly and casual with no agenda. But things really changed after we spent a wonderful week on Capri in February. Since then, we've seen each other every weekend."

"What's he like?"

"Oh, he's such a gentleman. He sends me flowers, little gifts, and writes sweet notes that he misses me. Notes on real paper, not texts or emails."

"The old-fashioned way of romance; I like that," Antonella said. "Who gets letters anymore when everyone sends emails or texts on your phone? Remember the old days? You'd receive a letter, open it with a little excitement, read it a few times. Even memorize the better lines if it's from a special boy—or man."

Rosanna laughed. "Oh, those were the days of romance and wondering where that special guy was when you didn't see him for a couple of days. Then, if he was thoughtful, he'd send a letter. You'd rip it open, read it a dozen times, and stuff it in a drawer to take out anytime you were lonely."

"Rosanna, you're such a romantic!" Antonella said, enjoying their spontaneity. "I remember those times, but they seem so long ago.

Unfortunately, today we're overwhelmed with technology that smothers us."

"So true," Rosanna said. "We've lost the intimacy of writing letters. Now, we get an email or text and delete it. Not Roberto—he sends me a note on special stationery at least once a week. Sometimes twice."

"That shows how much he cares for you. Does he want to get serious?"

"Maybe," Rosanna said, her voice drifting off, looking away. "But I have a problem with his . . . circumstances."

"What do you mean?"

"His hotel is owned by *camorristi*. I'm sure they launder money through it from selling drugs."

"Really?"

"Yes," she said, lowering her voice. "The hotel has accounts with our bank, and I check their cash flow. They don't deposit large amounts of cash, which would tip off the Guardia di Finanza. Instead, deposits tend to grow during the week, with larger amounts on weekends and holidays. What you might expect."

Rosanna looked over her shoulder to make sure no one was eavesdropping. "But I dug a little deeper. I calculated the hotel rates per night, per room, and the total if they were full. Since most guests pay with credit cards, cash deposits are small. But some nights, more cash comes in and is deposited the next day. On those nights, the hotel is not full, so they deposit more cash as if the hotel were full and guests paid in cash."

"Have you told your bank inspectors or the Guardia di Finanza?"

Rosanna shook her head. "No, I don't want to get involved. I could get in trouble with my employer." She looked over her shoulder again, but no one was within earshot. "I also recognize the names of owners," she continued. "One or two have been involved in criminal cases with other businesses in Campania—hotels, restaurants, resorts, waste-disposal companies. The Guardia di Finanza investigated them a few years ago and took them to court for money laundering. You know what happens then—hearings, motions for delays, those cases go on and on."

"Are you saying Roberto might be part of the *sistema*?"

"I don't know. He says he isn't, but his brother is a lawyer and has defended *camorristi* charged with illegally dumping hazardous chemical waste along roads —mercury, zinc, horrible stuff like that near schools in Caserta. Several children got sick walking home. Some chemicals spilled on the road and the children got it on their clothes and shoes. They ended up in the hospital; one almost died. And there's a cancer epidemic around Acerra, where *camorristi* have been dumping toxins on farmlands, poisoning crops, contaminating wells with lead, arsenic, and mercury."

"It's tragic how the land is being poisoned," Antonella said. "It's illegal, immoral, and criminal. I wish the government could enact stronger environmental laws. But the *camorristi* bribe politicians. Look how many have gone to jail the last few years." She stopped, not wanting to reveal classified information she'd learned at DIGOS. Antonella knew more than she was saying, but Camorra bribery cases had been published in newspapers or reported on TV. She was more interested in Rosanna's personal situation.

"So, you're being cautious before getting more involved with Roberto?" she asked.

Rosanna nodded. "I am; I don't want anything to do with criminals. I have a friend who married a *camorrista* but didn't know it. She thought he was a manager at a construction company. When he was arrested, she learned that he had been lying about his job. He worked for a shell company that owned the construction business, and he bribed politicians for government contracts for road improvements around Campania."

"What did she do?"

"She wants to divorce him. They don't have any children, thank God, but you know what it's like to get a divorce. Italia is still a very Catholic country; divorce is like a sin."

Their waiter arrived with their orders, plates of arugula salad, marinated anchovies, *fiorilli* (deep-fried, batter-coated zucchini flowers), and grilled calamari.

When the waiter left, Rosanna asked, "Do you know much about the *sistema?*"

Antonella nodded, feeling uneasy about revealing what she knew as a police officer. "You probably know that DIGOS isn't involved in mafia investigations, but I follow police reports about the Sicilian mafia, 'Ndrangheta, and Camorra. They've all infiltrated in the north, laundering money, buying hotels, resorts, restaurants, and shopping centers."

"How was your brother involved?"

"He was in a clan in Pianura feuding with a rival family selling drugs between Soccavo and Pianura. Salvo had a temper and liked to argue. What I learned was that he taunted members of the rival clan, called them obscene names. He even got into fights."

"I'm sorry. You two were so different. It's hard to believe that you were related."

"We were as different as night and day. So, while I'm here, I'm trying to learn more about his life. I met Salvo's business partner today; they ran a motorcycle shop in Pianura, no doubt financed by the Rocco clan's drug sales. I saw him at a pizzeria last night when he rescued me from a gang of boys trying to steal my purse and push me into the street."

"Really? Pianura is dangerous! Be careful. Were you frightened?"

"Yes, but I'm trying not to be. I have to go there to see Carmela and the family. The funeral is tomorrow in Pianura. The commissario told me they don't expect trouble at the funeral, but they'll have police along the procession to the cemetery."

"When are you going back to Milano?"

"Friday. That gives me a little more time to spend with Carmela and the children. I'd like to help the family start a new life, maybe leave Napoli."

"Bless you. I hope you can."

* * * * *

When Antonella returned to her hotel, she texted Carlo. It was 10 p.m. in Napoli, 8 a.m. in Sydney. He called her immediately.

"*Cara*, good morning. How are you?" He asked, his tone cheerful, a pleasant greeting that made Antonella smile.

She answered with a similarly warm response. "Oh, it's so nice to hear your voice, Carlo. I just got back from dinner with Rosanna, my banker friend."

"Wonderful. How is she?"

She related the dinner conversation with Rosanna, the afternoon meeting with Francesco, the previous night with Carmela's family at Vesuvio, and the unpleasant experience of the attempted purse snatching. He listened without interrupting, letting her express the range of emotions she felt, from fear of the incident to relief at connecting with the family and sharing pleasant memories with Rosanna.

When she was finished relating the events in Napoli, she asked, "Caro, I have a question. Do you think we could help Carmela and her family?"

"I suppose so. What do you have in mind?"

"I'm still thinking about it. Luisa plays the violin very well. I was impressed. Diego, on the other hand, is a bit of a rebel, but he likes to make pizza at the pizzeria where Carmela works. He says he wants to become a chef. If they came to Milano, I could arrange violin lessons for Luisa. Maybe we could help Diego get cooking lessons at a restaurant. You have good friends who manage restaurants."

"I do. When I get back, I'll contact them and see what they say. How about Carmela—does she want to leave Napoli?"

"She's lost without Salvo. We talked a little at Vesuvio last night. She confided in me, admits she's struggling. I'll draw her out more after the funeral. Hopefully, she'll tell me what she wants to do."

"It's tomorrow, right?"

"Yes. Then we'll go to Vesuvio for the wake. My last chance to see Carmela will be Friday morning. I hope we have time to talk about her future."

"Don't push it; it's her life. She has decisions to make. She's lived in Napoli her whole life. Could she leave her family and friends?"

"I don't know . . . I don't know. But I'll have to find out."

CHAPTER NINE

THURSDAY

Antonella and Carmela's family waited in De Cataldo's Mercedes behind the hearse parked in front of the Parrocchia San Giuseppe Operaio church. The hearse driver opened the back door and slid out Salvo's casket. Four pallbearers, including Francesco, grasped the handles and wheeled the simple casket toward the church entrance.

Their driver opened the passenger door to let Carmela's family out of the limousine. Antonella exited, smoothing a hand over her black pantsuit. Luisa emerged clutching a small purse and wearing a long black dress that reached the tops of her shiny black shoes. Diego almost tripped getting out. He fiddled with a coat that seemed too tight and ran a finger inside the collar of his white shirt. Carmela said something to him, and he stopped fidgeting.

Antonella took Luisa's hand, letting Carmela and Diego walk ahead. The family approached the church, nodding to older women, teenage girls, and mothers with young children who bowed and made signs of the cross as the family passed.

Among the mourners, Antonella recognized familiar faces from Vesuvio: two men who had been drinking Sambuca at the bar, a waiter, and the waitress who had served them Tuesday night.

A crowd of men slouched with arms folded across their chests stood in the shade of a tall magnolia tree, the ground littered with dried leaves and seed pods. One clenched his fists, spat on the ground, and rubbed it into the dirt with his heel. The Leone clan—all men—showed no visible signs of mourning. Antonella studied their faces as the family walked past, trying to read their intention for coming to Salvo's funeral.

She sensed tension between the Vesuvio mourners and the men under the magnolia tree. Commissario Belmondo had told her, "It's customary for rival families to attend funerals as a sign of respect, even if they were involved in the crime."

Mourners bowed and genuflected as Salvo's casket rolled past them to the church entrance, where a priest in white robes waited. He sprinkled holy water over the casket, mumbled a prayer, then led the pallbearers into the church. Two enormous wreaths stood near the entrance with the names of the Rocco and Leone families on their purple ribbons.

Antonella and Carmela's family followed inside the church, their eyes adjusting to the darkness from the bright sunlight. A black priest, possibly Nigerian, met them, made the sign of the cross, and led them down the center aisle as an organ played the opening chords of somber Bach interludes.

The priest led the family to the front pew. Salvo's casket, his name engraved on a metal plaque affixed to it, was draped with funeral wreaths, bouquets of lilies, red roses, purple irises, and banners printed with the names of the donors. Filing into the pew, Carmela followed Diego, who clutched his mother's hand. Luisa and Antonella followed Carmela. They bowed in silent prayer and then took their seats.

Two golden candles cast twin cones of light over the altar and Salvo's casket. Mourners shuffled into the church and took their places in the wooden pews as the organ played the traditional funeral concerto, Bach's *Toccata and Fugue in D Minor*, accented with powerful, mournful chords.

Altar boys in white robes walked down the center aisle, lighting candles on the ends of pews. Mourners hushed. The mood in the church grew somber as the sorrowful chords of the organ hung in the air like a heavy curtain. When the organ eventually stopped, the church was eerily quiet except for nervous coughs, a sneeze, and the shuffle of feet. A baby cried, followed by moments of uneasy tension until its mother rose from a pew, excused herself, and hurried outside.

Then silence.

The priest who had accompanied Salvo's casket emerged from behind a red curtain behind the altar, followed by two altar boys, one carrying a large gold cross and the other, an open Bible. The priest knelt, kissed the altar's white cloth, rose, and stretched out his arms for the mourners to stand. He made the sign of the cross and said, "Let us pray . . . we are gathered today to honor our dear departed brother, Salvatore Amoruso, and to remember all who have passed on to their heavenly reward."

The priest stepped down from the altar and approached the front pew. He placed a hand on Carmela's head, and then on Diego's and Luisa's, mumbling a prayer and signing the cross before each one.

Out of the corner of her eye, Antonella saw tears trickling down Carmela's cheeks, her chest heaving in and out. Diego's head was bowed so low his chin touched his chest, tears streaming down his cheeks. He dropped his mother's hand, wiped away tears, and grabbed Carmela's hand again.

Luisa leaned on her mother, sobbing, her damp and quivering hand still clutching Antonella's.

After a brief homily on the sanctity of the family, God's forgiveness, and the blessings of eternal life, the priest recited the Lord's Prayer as the mourners joined in. One of the pallbearers walked to the altar with a piece of paper. He read a brief biography of Salvo, called him a close friend, a loving father, and a man of honor who would be remembered by all.

Antonella cringed at the words "a man of honor," a term she despised for its sheer hypocrisy: condoning criminal actions, including murder, as a legitimate means of their "business" operations, as well as selling drugs, extorting other businesses, illegally dumping hazardous chemicals and poisoning the environment, and bribing politicians and government officials. All for criminal profits.

She closed her eyes, not wanting to endure the indignity. The reader left the altar and returned to the pew with the other pallbearers.

The priest paused and then walked around the altar to stand by Salvo's casket. The pallbearers rose from a side pew, walked to the casket, and gripped the handles. They shuffled a few small steps and pivoted to roll the casket down the aisle.

Mourners stood, making the sign of the cross as Salvo's casket passed down the aisle. The priest stood by the front pew with an open Bible in his hand and nodded at Carmela's family. They stood in unison. Antonella stepped out, letting Luisa, Carmela, and Diego pass in front of her. They followed the priest down the aisle as the organ began Chopin's *Funeral March*, a sad refrain evoking death and loss, the mournful chords rippling like falling tears. Mourners watched with sad eyes; women wept; men stared with blank faces.

They walked into the bright sunlight as the pallbearers slid Salvo's casket into the hearse. The driver pressed a button and the casket locked in place. The Leone men were still under the magnolia tree. None of them had entered the church or genuflected. Only stony stares.

Over an outdoor loudspeaker, the organ repeated Bach's *Toccata and Fugue in D Minor*, its chords rippling out over the departing mourners. It was a familiar ritual in the neighborhood: another funeral, another procession, a religious ceremony that kept churches and mortuaries busy.

A husky, clean-shaven man wearing a black sports coat with a police lapel button caught Antonella's eye. He stepped toward her and spoke in a low voice.

"Dottoressa Amoruso, my name is Gianfranco. Commissario Belmondo asked us to escort you." He turned to a younger man beside him, also wearing a black coat and police emblem. "This is Lorenzo; he'll be with us."

Antonella nodded. The younger officer took a few steps to stand next to Carmela. Antonella quietly said to Carmela, "We have a police escort to the cemetery."

Carmela looked at both men, a bit uneasily, and then nodded. "Thank you," she mumbled.

The hearse drove slowly away from the church, passing a building with funeral posters plastered on the wall announcing the demise of Salvo, listing the names of Carmela, Diego, Luisa, Antonella, and Marianna along with the day of his funeral. The hearse stopped for a moment, waiting for a flatbed truck carrying flowers from the church to join them.

The procession proceeded to Via Vicinale Campanile and turned left. Across from the church, uniformed officers stood in front of a police car, thumbs hooked onto wide black belts. Antonella recognized the husky woman who had escorted her to Belmondo's office; the officer caught Antonella's eye and acknowledged her with a nod.

The funeral procession started down the street with Carmela's family and their police escorts behind the hearse. Shops along the street had closed their shutters and turned off lights and music as the hearse and procession passed. The noon sun blazed down on the mourners as they followed the hearse. Shoppers and pedestrians watched the parade in silence; men took off their hats, women genuflected, children gawked.

At intersections, uniformed officers blocked traffic between the church and the cemetery. They scanned the crowd looking for signs of trouble. Gawkers watched from apartment balconies, drawn by the mournful organ music coming from the church loudspeaker. On vacant buildings, more posters of Salvo.

Three blocks from the church, the hearse turned a corner toward the cemetery. Antonella glanced behind at the long line that reached back to the church. A silent group, mourners staring ahead or at the ground, mothers holding children's hands, all shuffling toward the cemetery.

BLAM! A gunshot exploded, the sound reverberating off stores and apartments.

Antonella whipped her head around, saw a man in the procession fall.

BLAM! Another gunshot.

The procession became a stampede as screaming mourners ran for safety.

CHAPTER TEN

Antonella grabbed Luisa's arm, pulling her to the asphalt. "Get down!" She shouted at Carmela and Diego, who turned to look back. Antonella reached across Luisa, grabbed Diego's leg and pulled him down. He grunted and fell next to his sister.

"Heads down! Don't look up!"

Carmela turned around at the sound of the gunshots with a stunned look frozen on her ashen face. She covered her mouth.

"Nooooo!" she screamed.

"Down, Carmela!" Antonella lurched across Luisa and Diego to grasp Carmela's dress, tugging until Carmela slumped, falling forward, hands smacking the pavement.

"Stay down; don't look back!" Antonella barked, lying across Luisa and Diego's backs. Pandemonium on the street—children crying, women screaming, men yelling, fleeing in all directions. In the frenzied chaos, mourners fell to the asphalt, tripping others. Within seconds, bodies lay like human logs strewn across the street, littered with discarded purses, sunglasses, black shawls, scarves, and children's dolls.

A chorus of panicked screams.

"Help!"

"Police!"

"No!"

Police sirens screeched. Flashing red lights swept over the fleeing mourners. Officers wearing bulletproof vests bolted from cars, ran into the street, crouching and aiming pistols and military-style automatic weapons, searching for anyone holding a gun.

Some mourners found temporary shelter under tables outside coffee shops, behind benches, in doorways. Others splayed on the street, hands over their heads, screaming.

Two more gunshots, one on each side of the street. More screaming. Police ran toward the sounds of the gunshots.

Antonella glanced back at their police escorts. Gianfranco crouched by the hearse, aiming his service weapon with both hands, sweeping it across the fleeing crowds. Lorenzo was kneeling beside Carmela, holding his weapon in the air.

Antonella reached under her coat for her holster. She flipped off the leather strap, pulled out her Beretta pistol, pointing the barrel up.

Diego looked over at her and shouted, "Zia! Help!"

"Down!" She answered, pushing his head to the asphalt.

Antonella's eyes swept over the chaos, searching for someone not running, possibly with a weapon. Two men hadn't joined the fleeing mourners, Francesco and the waiter from Vesuvio, several meters behind the hearse. They both held small pistols, looking left, right, for shooters in the pandemonium.

Behind Francesco, a man lay on the street, a hand clutching his side, blood soaking his shirt. Francesco pushed the waiter toward the injured man. He ran, almost tripping over a mourner, to reach the man pressing on his wound.

Antonella scanned both sides of the street, her eyes like beacons searching for a possible shooter. Motion in a barbershop doorway caught her attention. A man crouched in the shadows, a pistol gripped in his hands.

"Shooter in barbershop!" she shouted at Lorenzo, pointing toward the man.

"Where?" Lorenzo was five yards from Antonella on her right, kneeling alongside Carmela.

"There!" she shouted again, pointing.

Out of the corner of her eye, she saw Francesco kneel and point his pistol toward the barbershop. The man in the barbershop fired a split second later, but the bullet missed Francesco and shattered a café window. Francesco aimed and fired back, exploding the barbershop window.

Antonella fired one shot into the doorway, the bullet thudding into the door inches from the shooter's chest.

The barbershop shooter swiveled to see where the shot had come from and saw Lorenzo sprinting toward him. He aimed and—

BLAM!

Antonella shot again. The shooter fell against a wall, blood erupting from his shoulder. Lorenzo reached the doorway, stomped on the shooter's hand, kicked the gun away, and jammed the barrel of his pistol to his head.

"Help!" Luisa screamed, covering her ears from Antonella's gunshots.

"Antonella, they're shooting at us!" Carmela shouted.

"Heads down! I'm here!" Antonella yelled.

A thunderous noise, like rockets blasting off from a missile range, muted the screaming, sirens, and gunshots. A blue police helicopter came into view from the entrance to the cemetery, its spear-like blades slicing through the air, black fumes belching from exhaust pipes. The engine's deafening noise ricocheted off buildings and the street below.

Antonella looked up; the pilot in the domed cockpit was wearing a black helmet like an alien from a distant planet. The pilot executed a slow semi-circle above the street, pausing in front of the hearse. Two gunners wearing similar helmets crouched in an open door of the helicopter, aiming 5.7 caliber automatic weapons below. The whirling blades kicked up a whirlwind of dusty debris—newspapers, discarded plastic bags, twigs, leaves, and paper coffee cups.

Terrified mourners clamped hands over their ears to shield themselves from the thunderous roar and clouds of sooty debris raining down on them. Their panicked breathing made them inhale dust and exhaust fumes into their lungs, choking them. Men, women, and children urinated in their clothes, cowering in fear. Bowels opened.

Gritty debris and dust swept over Antonella, Carmela, Luisa, and Diego, getting into their hair, nostrils, ears, and eyes. They coughed, wheezed, closed their eyes.

"Oh God, oh God, help us!" Carmela shouted between gasps.

Luisa screamed, "Help! Help!"

"Zia—I'm scared!" Diego cried out, ending in a coughing spasm.

Two police cars sped around the corner in front of the cemetery, tires burning rubber, sirens screaming, red lights flashing. They braked inches from the hearse's front bumper. Helmeted police officers wearing bulletproof vests leaped from the cars, ran down the street with automatic weapons in firing position. They ignored Antonella and Carmela's family behind the hearse, stepped over mourners on the ground, ran to benches where some had found temporary refuge.

The helicopter, with its oily fumes spewing from exhaust pipes, passed slowly over the hearse and followed the police running toward the church. The helicopter swiveled deliberately, its whirring blades sweeping debris from rooftops, raining down twigs, dried leaves, and cigarette butts over the huddled mourners.

More screaming sirens arrived near the church. Three vehicles turned the corner, including RAI and Napoli news vans with TV antennas on the roof. They screeched to a halt; cameramen jumped out and began running toward the mourners, filming them as they fled. Behind the TV vans, an ambulance pulled up: white-coated medical personnel exited and ran into the crowds, carrying satchels of medical equipment, kneeling to comfort fallen mourners and those huddled under benches.

The gunshots ceased. But not the cacophony of whirring helicopter blades, sirens, flashing red lights, people screaming for help.

Chaos gradually declined from panic to tension. Police radios squawked. Officers lowered weapons. The helicopter rose and flew over an apartment, hovering but not departing. Door gunners still searched the crowds for shooters.

Red lights flashed, but there were no more gunshots. Screaming gave way to crying and whimpered pleas for aid. Teams of police secured the area, looked in doorways, at apartment rooftops, alleys, and parked cars, communicating with microphones attached to their bulletproof vests, relaying status reports and listening to commands from superiors.

Antonella surveyed the changing scenario, counting how many gunshots she had heard. Two before chaos erupted, another two, then two or three from Francesco and the barbershop shooter, and her two gunshots. Was it eight, nine? But none since she had wounded the barbershop shooter.

The danger seemed to have passed. Police patrolled the street, searching in vain for shooters. None appeared; the incident seemed to have been limited to one or two random shooters, not a calculated assault on mourners. While Antonella watched the teams of police, she sensed they had secured the area. She holstered her weapon and pulled her suit coat over it.

Antonella stood up, eyes still scanning the street as she helped Carmela, Diego, and Luisa to stand and brush debris from their clothes and hair. They rubbed their eyes, blew noses, coughed, and spit up phlegm.

"Are we safe?" Diego asked, his voice quavering.

"Yes, I think so. Just stay here."

Francesco tucked his pistol into a holster behind his back and started walking toward the family, brushing off his black pants and coat. Carmela saw him, put a hand to her mouth.

"Are you OK, Francesco?"

"Yes, I'm fine."

When he was close, she reached out and grabbed his arm.

"What happened? Who was shooting? Why?" she cried.

"I don't know; it started back there," he said, turning around and pointing to where the police were talking to mourners who were gesturing at doorways and toward the church, talking excitedly about where the shots had come from.

He looked at Antonella.

"*Mio Dio,* you saved me, *signora,*" he said, his voice quavering. Beads of sweat on his forehead were dripping on his cheeks. "He . . . he was aiming at me, . . . and you shot him."

She ignored his comment. "Where's your family? Are they all right?"

"They didn't come today," he said. "Our baby was sick, up all night; my wife wanted to be with her."

"Good. They're safe."

Francesco was going to say something, but Gianfranco came over to Antonella. She turned her back to Francesco, not wanting to talk to him.

"Who's that?" Gianfranco asked.

"A pallbearer . . . Salvo's business partner. Don't worry about him."

"Are you OK? You shot the guy in the barbershop."

"I'm fine—don't worry about me. What do you know?"

"Commissario Belmondo said they arrested two shooters, and another suspect was seen running down an alley; they're after him."

"Good. Can you stay here with the family? I have to go over there," she said, pointing toward the barbershop.

"Of course."

Antonella turned back to the family, "This officer will stay with you. I have to talk to the escort over there," she said pointing toward the barbershop, where Lorenzo and two other officers were standing over the man she had shot.

"Are you sure?" Carmela asked. "I'm afraid. What if—"

"Don't worry, I think the danger's passed. The police arrested two, and they're chasing another," she answered.

Antonella put her arms around Diego and Luisa and pulled them close. "You're OK?"

They nodded. "Yes, I think so," Luisa mumbled. Diego looked like he was about to cry but was holding back.

"Police have secured the area; medics are checking those who might have been injured," she said as she scanned the crowd and saw nurses examining faces, arms, hands for cuts and scratches. Emergency personnel carried stretchers and medical kits to those struggling to stand, asking if they needed help. Rescuers lifted a black-shawled old woman onto a gurney and rolled it to a waiting ambulance. Another team helped a mother cradling a child to a temporary aid station.

"How do you feel?" she asked.

"I can't believe it . . ." Luisa whimpered. "Why . . . did this happen? I'm scared!"

"Me, too," Diego stammered. "Don't leave us, Zia. Stay here, please."

Antonella looked over at the barbershop doorway, where three police officers and Lorenzo were standing over the wounded shooter. Lorenzo looked over and signaled to her.

"Stay here; I have to go there," she said to Carmela and the children. She motioned for Gianfranco. "This officer will stay with you. I'll be back in a minute."

Antonella walked to the barbershop, eyes darting left and right for signs of danger. Lorenzo said something to the senior officer, who turned around as she approached. The shooter lay on the ground, clutching his arm, blood soaking his shirt. A medical technician kneeled and checked his pulse.

When she reached the barbershop, she heard the medical technician say, "He's lost a lot of blood. We'll get him into the ambulance."

Technicians wheeled a gurney toward the barbershop. The police stepped back and let the techs lift him onto the gurney. One poked a needle into the suspect's arm to begin a blood transfusion. When the plastic bag of blood and the transfusion line were in place, the aides tightened belts across his chest and legs before wheeling the gurney from the doorway, rotating it to return to the ambulance.

Lorenzo turned to the ranking officer. "Sir, this is Dottoressa Amoruso from Milano. She's DIGOS. She wounded him before he could shoot me."

Antonella nodded but didn't respond.

The senior officer studied her face and asked, "You have ID?"

She reached into her purse, pulled out her DIGOS identification, and handed it over. He examined it and looked at her face to match it to the photo on her badge. He handed it back and said, "Giorgio Lucchini your boss?"

"Yes, he knows I'm here. We talked this morning. I'll call him and report what happened."

The officer nodded. "Commissario Belmondo will want a statement from you, too."

"Of course," she nodded. "I'll go to the station tomorrow."

The officer squinted, a puzzled look on his face. "What were you—"

Lorenzo interrupted, answering the officer's question.

"Sir, the *dottoressa* is Salvo's family."

"What?

"That's right; he was my half-brother . . . same father," Antonella answered. "I'm with his family," she said, nodding at Carmela's family behind the hearse.

"OK, OK, but you better leave before the media finds you," he said, nodding toward the Canale 21 TV cameraman and reporter heading toward the barbershop. "They're turning this place into a circus," he snarled. "Don't let them question you."

"I won't," Antonella said and then turned to Lorenzo. "Will you help me get the family to my hotel, where they'll be safe? I don't want TV cameras near them."

"Of course."

She and Lorenzo started back to the hearse where Carmela, Luisa, and Diego stood silently watching. Antonella reached out to take Carmela's arm.

"We're going to my hotel. This officer will drive us there."

"Why the hotel?" Diego asked.

"You'll be safe there. Let's go."

She glanced back and saw the cameraman and reporter trying to catch up with them.

CHAPTER ELEVEN

Lorenzo drove Antonella and Carmela's family to the International Hotel. When they entered her room, Diego dashed to grab the remote and turned on the TV. He flicked through channels and found the RAI 24 station rebroadcasting segments from the funeral procession. A young, blonde female reporter was interviewing witnesses, medical teams, and police officers while the camera panned the now empty street cordoned off with yellow police tape.

"Look, look," Diego cried out. "That's us . . . we're leaving! That's our car!"

The TV camera had recorded Lorenzo's police car as it departed from the church as the reporter spoke somberly.

"The family of Salvatore Amoruso, the Camorra member murdered two years ago, is leaving the scene of a deadly shooting during the funeral procession. We have a witness who was in the church and in the procession—"

"Turn that off, Diego!" Carmela grabbed the remote and punched the off button. "That isn't a stupid crime show; that's us. Today! You're not watching this!"

"Mamma, I want to," he begged.

"No! No TV!" She stuffed the remote in her purse and reached for her cigarettes. "I need a cigarette . . . I need to calm down."

"On the balcony, please," Antonella said. "The hotel has 'no smoking in rooms' signs posted."

"Sure . . . sure," Carmela said, opening the patio sliding glass door, purse in one hand, a cigarette dangling from her lips.

Luisa lay on the bed and stretched. "Oh, this bed is so comfortable. Can I lie here, Zia?"

"Sure, you can. Relax. We all need a rest."

Luisa took off her shoes and kicked them away. "This is a nice room," she said. "I wish we could stay here tonight."

"I'll ask your mother if I should get you a room."

"Nah, I don't think Mamma would let us," Luisa said. "Besides, I think we'll all want to be home tonight. Right, Diego?"

"No, let's stay here. This is a cool place, better than our crappy apartment," Diego said, texting on his phone. "I'll invite my friends to come."

"No, don't do that, Diego," Luisa said. "Stop texting; don't tell anyone where we are."

"But I want to see them," he pleaded.

"Not now—see them tomorrow."

"Hey, you're sounding like Mamma now, not my sister. She never lets me do what I want to do," he said, pouting.

"Stop it. And don't complain about our apartment; we have a nice home. You have a bedroom, all your music, computer games. What else would you want?"

"Nah, I'm bored with our home. Nothing ever changes . . . we've lived in the same apartment our whole lives. I want to move, maybe get an apartment close to the bay and the islands. That's where I want to live, near a beach so I can go swimming every day with my friends. We're sick of Pianura; it's just a crummy suburb, so boring."

"That's mean, Diego; you're so negative, never happy with anything," Luisa said. "And your friends, I don't like any of them. Get some new ones."

"Oh, shut up. You don't know what you're talking about," he answered.

Antonella felt like she was eavesdropping on a continuing drama between Diego and Luisa. He was growing more independent from his sister and mother—typical behavior for an adolescent—while Luisa was the responsible older sister, loyal to her mother and trying to restrain her brother's rash impulses.

Antonella watched Diego texting on his mobile phone, tuning Luisa out, more concerned with his friends, where they were, what they were doing and saying than what his sister was saying. In his mind, he was miles away, not with his mother, sister, and *zia* in a three-star hotel as a captive of social media.

On the balcony, Carmela snuffed out her cigarette, blew out smoke, and re-entered the apartment. "Hey, what's going on? Diego, quit texting; you'll go blind staring at screens all day."

"Mamma, that's not true," Luisa said. "You're on your phone a lot, too. And your computer."

"Please, let's not—" Carmela started, but Antonella interrupted.

"Is anybody hungry?" she asked, sensing a need to insert herself into the dynamics of the moment, which was turning out to be more of an unraveling than a uniting after the funeral. She sensed Diego and Luisa would gang up on their mother, and it would strain an already tense family situation. They were just an hour removed from Salvo's funeral, less than that from the shooting, and the family was quarreling as if nothing had happened that morning.

They needed a pause in the conflicting emotions of grief, fear, and loss, a few moments to heal.

"I'll call the hotel restaurant, have them send up water and sandwiches," Antonella said.

"Caffè, please. I want caffè," Carmela said.

"Luisa, what would you like?"

She shook her head. "I don't know, maybe something to drink. Orange soda or a Coke. I'm not hungry."

"Diego?"

"Can we get a pizza?" Diego asked, not looking up from his mobile.

Antonella looked at Carmela, who nodded.

"Sure, go ahead."

"Margherita, extra mozzarella," Diego said. "Get me an orange Fanta. And biscotti."

Luisa added, "Maybe I do want something since Diego's getting pizza. How about a *tramezzino*?"

Antonella called room service and placed an order.

"Thirty to forty minutes," she said. "I think it will be closer to forty-five."

"I'm starving!" Diego said.

"Check the refrigerator," Antonella said. "They have candy bars and soft drinks. Take what you want."

"Yeah!" He dropped his mobile on the bed and opened the small refrigerator.

"Do they have Sprite?" Luisa asked, getting up from the bed and opening the sliding glass door to the balcony. "Bring it outside if they have it. I want fresh air."

"Yeah, they do. Fanta. Coke, too," Diego said. "Anybody want something?"

"No, thanks," Antonella said.

"Give me a Coke," Carmela said. "Diet, if they have it."

"Hey, look what else they have in here—candy! Ferrero Rocher, my favorite chocolate!" he said, ripping off the wrapping and tossing it on the floor.

"Diego, pick that up; you're making a mess."

"All right, all right," he said as he grabbed the wrapper and threw it onto the bed.

"In the garbage can, not the bed," she said.

"Aw, Mamma," he complained, tossing the wrapper into a garbage can next to the TV.

Diego handed a can of Sprite to Luisa on the balcony and a Diet Coke to his mother. He popped the top on his Coke, sat back on the bed, and grabbed his phone.

Luisa said, "Look, Diego, there's a pool down there. Cool. It's nice out here. Zia Antonella, this is a beautiful view! I love this! Look how big the bay is . . . all that blue water. It's beautiful. And all the ships! And Vesuvio, it looks bigger here."

"We're closer to it, silly," Diego said, going out on the balcony, standing next to his sister.

"You kids are doing what I do every day when I come back to the hotel," Antonella said as she joined them, wanting to be positive. "I go out on the balcony, gaze at the panorama of the Bay, Vesuvio, Capri, Ischia, and islands to the south. You're lucky to live in such a beautiful part of Italia."

"I don't think Napoli is so beautiful—" Diego started to protest before Luisa cut him off.

"Stop being negative, Diego! Say something nice for a change. Listen to Zia; this *is* a beautiful scene from her balcony."

Luisa leaned over the railing, staring down. "Oh, Zia, look at your pool . . . I wish we could go swimming."

Antonella stayed in the balcony doorway, patting Luisa on the back. "Yes, it is beautiful. If you had a suit, you could go in."

Inside the room, Carmela said, "Diego, I want to talk to you."

"What do you want?" He scowled. "I like it out here with Luisa and Zia."

"How do you feel about today . . . about what happened?" Carmela asked.

"It was bad, Mamma, very bad. I was scared, real scared. I was afraid someone might shoot us."

"Zia Antonella was there for us; she kept us safe," Carmela said as Diego turned to look at Antonella.

"I know that. Thanks, Zia," he said, looking more like a vulnerable adolescent than a strong-willed teenager. "I was going to run, but you grabbed me and pulled me down. I guess we were safer lying on the street than running, don't you think, Zia?"

"I do," Antonella looked at Diego and saw an insecure boy, not a soon-to-be young man demanding independence. Looking at Diego up close, she almost felt like it was Salvo in front of her when he was fourteen, just before he stole the Vespa and began his downward spiral into criminal activities. Salvo was emotionally vulnerable as an adolescent, living two lives, one with his father and his family and the other with his aunt and uncle. What would happen to Diego, losing his father as a teenager and facing an uncertain future? Would Carmela remarry, and if so, would he get along with his step-father? Diego's world would change dramatically in the next few years. How would he adjust? Would he adjust well or become full of rage as his father had?

"Diego, it was horrible what happened today," Carmela said. "We could have—"

He interrupted his mother. "My friend Pasquale was there, close to one of the people shooting."

"I don't care about Pasquale; I care about you and your sister!"

"Oh, Mamma," he groaned. "Don't do that again. Can't we just be here without all the talking? You're so *borrrring.*"

Luisa came back into the room. "Mamma, can I go for a walk? I want to go down to the pool; people are swimming. There's a café and a patio. It looks like fun; I want to go there and see the children swim."

"Take your brother with you."

"Yeah, let's go—it's boring in the hotel," Diego said, stuffing his phone in his coat pocket.

"Don't leave the hotel. Diego, hear me?"

"Yeah, Mamma, OK. When will my pizza be here?"

* * * * *

"I'll call and have them deliver in an hour. No need to rush," Antonella said.

They left the room, and Carmela reached into her purse and took out her cigarettes.

"I need another cigarette. Do you mind?"

"Not at all, go ahead."

She took out a cigarette and went onto the balcony, lighting up with a plastic lighter. Antonella followed, standing beside her.

Carmela took a deep drag, tilting back her head and exhaling a plume of smoke. Her hands were shaking until she grabbed the railing. She took another drag, exhaled, and closed her eyes. When she opened them, she spoke without looking at Antonella.

"God, what a horrible day. I can't believe it; you think you'd be safe at a funeral. But then crazies—people with guns . . ."

She turned to Antonella. "Didn't you used to smoke?"

"Yes."

"You quit?"

"Four years ago. It wasn't easy."

"Good for you. I should quit. I smoke two packs a day."

"It would be good if you quit."

Carmela looked at her cigarette, took a puff. "But not now. I have too much on my mind. My life's crazy. Salvo is dead. I'm worried about the children . . . afraid every day. What do you think I should do?"

Antonella was encouraged. Carmela was confiding in her as a close friend, seeking advice about critical life issues. The distance, aloofness of the past, was gone.

"It depends, Carmela. What would you like to do?" Antonella started with an open-ended question. Not offering advice, just seeking more information.

Carmela huffed in an expression of frustration.

"Make changes. I'm going to be forty next month. A widow with two independent teenagers. Very independent! They need me now, but in a couple years, they'll be living someplace else. I'll be alone. Working at Vesuvio."

She shuddered, took another drag, her fingers still twitching. Carmela looked for an ashtray, and not finding one, she leaned down, flicked the ash onto the balcony tile.

"I'm stuck, Antonella. A middle-aged widow—with no future."

Another drag, another cough. She cursed.

"*Vaffanculo!* I gotta quit these damn cigarettes!" She dropped the cigarette onto the balcony, snuffed it out with her shoe, and looked at Antonella, her eyes bloodshot. "Talk to me, Antonella," she pleaded, opening her arms. They embraced, Carmela pressing close, the smell of cigarette smoke in her hair.

They held their embrace. Carmela sniffled, letting out a long sigh, her chest sagging, expanding. When she pulled away, she looked at Antonella, their faces inches apart.

"You're exhausted, Carmela. You need rest."

"I need more than that. I'm . . . having a nervous breakdown. Even my brother and his wife deserted me. I can't even count on my family when I need them! What kind of family deserts a widow at the funeral of her husband?" she said, spitting out the words.

"I'm sorry," Antonella said. "Luisa mentioned they were coming on Tuesday—"

"But he canceled at the last minute! Can you believe that? He texted that he twisted his knee and couldn't walk. How lame! I don't think he even booked a flight. He always has excuses like that. He didn't even come when Salvo disappeared, although I almost begged him." Carmela was on the verge of tears.

"I'm so sorry," Antonella empathized as she took Carmela's hands in her own.

"You see why I'm upset? I don't have *any* family to fall back on . . . except you."

"I'm here for you. You need to talk; you have so much stress in your life."

"I'm trapped, Antonella," she pleaded.

"You've said that. What do you want?"

"I want to change! Everything! Now, please!"

She embraced Antonella again, sagging into her, her hands pressing into her back. When she pulled back, she was shaking. She turned away, looked down at the pool.

Carmela pointed below and laughed.

"Look, there are the kids."

Diego and Luisa were relaxing on lounge chairs near the children's pool, staring at their mobiles, but still talking.

"Damn, I wish they wouldn't spend so much time on their phones. They don't listen to me when I'm at home; they just talk on their phones. But that's kids these days."

Diego reached into his coat pocket, took out a pack of cigarettes, offered the pack to Luisa, who took one.

"Look, they're smoking!" Carmela said. "Diego gave Luisa a ciga-rette! I've told them a million times—smoking is bad! I don't want them to smoke!"

"They're OK, Carmela. They need time together. It's been a hard day for all of us. Let's go inside, you need to relax and not get excited." Antonella led her into the room and pulled up a chair to sit down. Carmela sat on the bed.

"This is better . . . I wish I had some wine. I need to calm down."

"Shall I call down to have them deliver a bottle?"

"No, no, we have to go to the wake soon. There'll be wine there."

"Lie down, take a nap if you want. You look exhausted."

Carmela shook her head. "I am, but I don't want a nap. I want to talk."

"Go ahead, you start."

"I can't believe I'm going to say this, but I have to."

"Go ahead."

"I want to leave Napoli. Soon."

Antonella nodded, wanting her to continue. "Is that the right thing to do . . . now?"

"Yes! I want to change my life. And the children's lives."

"How would you do that?"

"Go someplace far away from here."

"Where do you want to go?"

"Not Roma, too big, all the traffic. And immigrants. Small towns are boring. Too many tourists in Venezia and Firenze. Not Puglia . . . Sicilia."

"A lot of places you don't want," Antonella said.

"I want to go north. Milano maybe."

"I like it there. It could be a good place to consider."

"It's expensive, everyone knows that," Carmela said. "But that doesn't worry me; I have money . . . enough to get by for a while. Someone's buying Salvo's share of the motorcycle shop, so I'll have more money. With that, I can get an apartment where it's not too expensive."

"Milano has nice suburbs. Monza is less than an hour from Milano. People commute every day into Milano."

"Salvo went to Monza for a race; he said he liked it. There's a big park there."

"Yes, but there are other towns a little further away . . . Parma, Piacenza, Bergamo. All nice places to consider."

Carmela nodded. "I don't care; they all sound better than here."

"Would you get a job?"

"Of course, I can work in a restaurant. But what I'd like to do is go back to school, get my accounting degree, finally. I was studying accounting when I met Salvo and we married. I liked school. I read a lot, too . . . when I have time. Not much recently."

"Having a degree would open doors."

"I always wanted an education, that's what I tell the children, too. Luisa is probably going to uni . . . I don't know about Diego," she said, shaking her head. "Maybe he would, but he has to make changes in how he behaves."

"When do you want to leave Napoli?"

"Soon. I don't like the heat in summer; it's awful, hotter than hell, as you know."

"Not much better in Milano. But you can go up to the lakes—Como, Maggiore, Garda."

"Yes, I'll definitely go there. Get away, maybe do some hiking even." She laughed. "Listen to me; my husband's funeral was today, and I talk about wanting to go hiking. Am I crazy?"

"Not at all. You've been under a tremendous strain for two years."

"More than two years, believe me," she said shaking her head. "Much more."

Antonella let Carmela's statement linger. A depressing statement that Carmela was hinting about, a marriage that seemed to be challenging, raising two children with apparently little help from her husband. The danger of being in the grip of the *sistema,* the prospect of being arrested, imprisoned, or murdered.

Antonella felt she was witnessing the damage of criminal systems, be it the Camorra in Napoli, *Cosa Nostra* in Sicilia, or other criminal organizations in the south. The rewards might seem good financially, but with the *sistema* came constant fear, danger, and an uncertain future for anyone involved. Especially families and children. Carmela, Luisa, and Diego were the victims of a system that strangled everyone affiliated with it.

"How will you tell the children?"

She shook her head. "Don't worry, I can take care of that. Promise them a new life. They'd adjust, especially if they had something to do."

"Luisa could continue violin lessons," Antonella said. "I have a friend who plays in an orchestra. She teaches violin and cello in a youth symphony."

"Good."

"Diego can take cooking classes and when he's sixteen, maybe get a part-time job in a restaurant."

"Making pizzas," Carmela laughed. "He'd love that. But he needs to get serious about school. He's been in trouble, doesn't like to go."

"Maybe a new school . . . new friends. A different town."

Carmela nodded. She reached for her cigarettes, took out one, but tossed it back on the bed. "No more cigarettes; I need to quit."

Carmela stood up, walked back onto the balcony, looked down at the children and waved. "They're leaving; I think they're coming up."

She returned to the room, folding her arms across her chest.

"Antonella, we have a plan," she said with a feeble effort of a smile.

"You have a plan."

"You helped me."

"Just by listening to you, that's all I did," Antonella said softly.

"No one else listened before. Or cared about me. Shall I tell the children now?"

"Umm, I don't know. Maybe wait a little. It's been a stressful day. I leave tomorrow, maybe tell them after I leave."

Carmela shook her head. "No, I want them to know it's not just me making decisions; you were part of it. You're their *zia*. They like you and trust you. You're part of the family."

Carmela went out on the balcony again, leaned against the railing, and looked over Napoli's skyline as the sun was setting in the west, the last rays shining on Vesuvio, shimmering south of the Bay.

Carmela turned and came back into the room. For the first time since they had arrived, she looked content.

"OK, I'm ready to go," she said. "Once the kids are here, we'll go to Vesuvio for the wake. And drink some wine, I need a glass or two, how about you?"

Antonella nodded, watching Carmela raise a fist and make a faint punching motion, then she smiled.

"Whew, what a day," Carmela said. "I *never* want to go through that again."

The door opened as Luisa and Diego burst in.

"Beat you!" Diego said, making a face at his sister.

"*Ragazzi*. Look at them," Carmela said. "They'll always be children."

CHAPTER TWELVE

Three police cars were parked outside Vesuvio that night. Armed police stood by the cars, several yards from the front door, allowing guests to enter. Antonella parked across the street, and the family got out and walked to the entrance. Antonella nodded at the officers; one she recognized from the procession. Diego hurried to the front door and held it open.

The chatter of conversation and kitchen noise hushed when Carmela's family entered. No tinkling wine glasses or plates clattering, the audio from the TV soccer match was muted, animated comments about the shooting ceased. Carmela held Luisa's and Diego's hands, looking awkward in a social situation she was unsure she could manage.

Carmela's women friends recognized her distress; they scooted back their chairs and encircled the family, murmuring words of condolence, enveloping them in tearful hugs. One by one, the women embraced Carmela, shed tears, offered gentle kisses, held her hands. No sobbing or emotional outbursts; this was a family in need of soothing words and calm behavior.

Antonella sensed the grieving ritual was familiar to the wives and mothers; they were experienced in paying respect to mourning families with kind words about the deceased and prayers for a better future. Then, they'd step aside for the next mourner.

Antonella recognized women from the funeral, a few still wearing black dresses and scarves, in mourning for Salvo's family, but also for family members long deceased. Most likely they were wives, parents, or grandparents of Rocco men in the *sistema*.

Luisa and Diego eased away from the crowd around Carmela, moving to join friends sipping soft drinks and eating pizzas at tables near the kitchen. Luisa's friends greeted her with hugs; Diego's buddies slapped him on the back. Within moments, most had turned their attention to mobile phones; texting, talking, watching videos or taking selfies. The grieving ritual of a wake for a friend's father was but a momentary interruption in their digital world of gossip, escape, and entertainment. Death was boring. Let parents, relatives, old people, and the church deal with it. They weren't interested.

Vesuvio was coming alive again, resuming its animated atmosphere, just a bit more subdued. Wine glasses tinkled, plates clattered, harsh words of revenge were spoken about the Leone clan. Kitchen staff resumed preparing pizzas, pasta, and salads, as waiters and waitresses delivered platters, maneuvering around tables like skaters on ice.

Antonella stepped aside from the dwindling crowd around Carmela, looking for a place to sit. She spotted an empty table near the bar and made her way through the crowd, nodding at mourners she'd seen at the funeral.

She sat down, picked up a menu, and scanned it. All she wanted was a salad and a glass of wine, and then to return to her hotel to pack. She caught the attention of a passing waiter and ordered. When he departed, Antonella noticed Francesco with his wife at a table near the private room. He caught her eye and leaned over to say something to his wife. Antonella looked away, not wanting to talk to him or meet his wife.

The waiter returned and set the Prosecco and a small bottle of mineral water on her table. "Your salad will be coming soon, *signora*," he said before departing.

As she sipped her wine, she looked around the room, noticing women nodding at her, smiling respectfully. She smiled back with a polite nod, not wanting to socialize at the wake. It was not much of a secret who she was; she expected that word had traveled with lightning speed that Salvo's half-sister, a police officer from Milano, would be in their presence for a few days. The irony was not likely lost on any of them.

Pizza places were not Antonella's usual place to eat or socialize, but, after all, this was Napoli, world famous as the home of pizza, especially Margherita, named after the queen from Savoia. Antonella's mind wandered. She relaxed, sipped her wine, happy not to be responsible for anyone's security or comfort. In less than twenty-four hours, she would be back home in her own apartment. The thought was comforting.

The waiter delivered her salad. She picked up the fork and took a few bites. She wasn't that hungry but needed to eat something before she left. After another sip of wine, she looked across the room to where Carmela was drinking wine with a table full of women, engrossed in conversation, not grieving.

Antonella didn't notice a man approaching her table from the bar. His voice interrupted her.

"*Buona sera, signora*. May I join you?"

Antonella looked up. The priest from the funeral was by her side, holding a glass of red wine, dressed casually in a long-sleeved black shirt with a white clerical collar. Without the white collar, he could have been an uncle, father, or grandparent, looking confident and relaxed.

"Hello, Father," she said, starting to stand.

"No ceremony necessary. Please, may I join you?" he repeated.

"Of course, Father."

"My name is Vincenzo. The priest took a seat, blocking the view of Francesco and his wife.

"I hope you're not surprised to see me enjoying a glass of wine outside of church."

"Not at all, Father."

"It's permissible for priests to drink wine. It's in the Bible," he said, his eyes sparkling as if he had told a joke. "Jesus drank wine . . . so did the disciples. I'm sure you remember in the Bible, Jesus's first miracle was changing water into wine at a wedding in Cana."

He raised his glass; they clinked. "To a safer, more loving future for everyone, as God wants it," he toasted.

"Yes, a safer future," Antonella responded. They took sips and sat back in their chairs.

"What a pleasant surprise, Father. Thank you for coming over."

"I saw you come in with Carmela and the children," he said. "I'll go over and talk to her later. If you don't mind, could we share a few moments?" His manner was pleasantly casual and warm. Faint lines radiated from his eyes and the corners of his mouth. A priest with a personality, a nice change.

"Of course, Father, but you don't have to apologize; everyone should enjoy wine."

"We certainly do in Napoli. You're from Milano, I understand." His voice was soothing, a pleasant break from the noisy chatter and clatter of plates.

"That's right."

"And you're in the police?"

"DIGOS, *Divisione Investigazioni Generali e Operazioni Speciali.*"

"A worthy calling, protecting our nation from terrorists. How did you choose DIGOS?"

"I went to law school, got my first job in the Roma police, and then applied for DIGOS. I spent a year in training and was transferred to Milano, where I met my husband."

"Ah, Milano, one of my favorite cities in Italia. I return once a year to participate in services at the Duomo with priests I've known since seminary. I always manage to spend a few days on one of the lakes. Lake Como and Maggiore are my favorites."

"Same with me. The lakes are a beautiful part of Italia."

"We're so lucky to live in such a unique country, with so much history and beauty. And of course, the seat of the Catholic church in Roma. A beloved city; I participate in Vatican services, including Easter this year."

"I went to the Vatican many times when I lived in Roma," she said with a smile. "One of my uncles was a priest as well . . . but unfortunately, he died young, such a tragedy."

"I'm sorry. How did he die?"

"From a disease he picked up in Africa where he was a missionary."

"Oh, I'm so sorry. He died serving the Lord." He changed the subject. "I hope you don't mind, but could I ask you a somewhat personal question?"

"Of course."

"Did Salvo talk to you about your career?"

She frowned. "Almost every time I saw him. He was not happy that I was a police officer. But that was the career I chose, and I have no regrets. Unfortunately, he made other choices."

"Yes . . . unfortunately. Very sad."

"Could I ask you a personal question?" Antonella asked.

"Absolutely, I dislike conversations that are mere pleasantries. I yearn to know the deeper parts of people lives, spiritually and emotionally."

"Good. How well did you know Salvo?" she asked.

He sipped his wine, took a moment before he answered. "I knew Carmela first; she asked me to celebrate their marriage. I was introduced to Salvo during pre-marital counseling. Later, I baptized Luisa and Diego and served their first communions."

"You knew the family well, then."

"Quite well, in fact. In the early days of their marriage, Salvo came to confession once or twice, told me things in confidence. I cautioned him about his 'activities.' I sensed he didn't like what I said, and he stopped coming."

"You mean the activities of being part of the Rocco *sistema?*"

"Of course. I'm sure you know all about Camorra," he said, looking around the room, nodding at people who had been watching them.

Antonella nodded. "Yes, I do. But I'm not involved in police investigations in Napoli."

"I understand; you came here to be with the family, to offer them comfort while they grieve."

She nodded again.

"Good. Then I hope we can share our concerns about them," he said. "Are you comfortable talking with me about sensitive matters?"

"Yes, I am."

"I'm a priest, but please also consider me a close friend of Carmela's family."

She nodded, wanting him to continue.

"I'm concerned about them," he continued.

"So am I," Antonella said.

"There is a bit of urgency in this meeting. We may not see each other again. Let me start by saying I've served at many funerals of men like Salvo who died because of their . . . affiliations."

"In the Rocco *sistema,*" she said.

He nodded. "That . . . and others. It grieves me to see families devastated when a parent, a brother, a father is taken from us. The families rarely heal, the grief remains for a lifetime. I ask God why he allows it . . ." he said, shaking his head . . . "but nothing changes. More violence, more senseless deaths . . . it just never seems to cease."

"Anyone in the police is familiar with the devastation that criminals cause, whether it's simple robbery, or murder, or terrorism. People read the headlines about a crime, toss the paper away, and resume their lives. But crimes have unwitting casualties . . . wives, children, friends. They often never recover emotionally from the criminal acts of a family member."

He nodded, looked away, and then looked back. "How long will you be in Napoli?"

"I return tomorrow."

He grimaced. "Too bad. Carmela will need support in the weeks and months to come. Spouses bear a heavy burden in times like this."

"Children, as well," she added.

"You're right, I meant to include them. Carmela and the children will need emotional support from all of us," he said, "but especially from you . . . me . . . others you do not know."

Antonella nodded. "The family came to my hotel after the shooting today," she said. "Carmela and I had a serious talk about her future. Possibly about the same topics."

"I'm glad she did. She needs someone to confide in. I'm not at liberty to share private conversations with her. . . but I imagine we had a similar talk." He reached up and touched his white collar. "What you say won't go any further. This is just between us."

Antonella nodded, considering this a two-way confession, but not one conducted in church. She had not confessed to a priest for decades, not since she'd been a teenager. Father Vincenzo had initiated the conversation and was seeking her cooperation. She had no idea if this was within the scope of priestly duties, but she didn't care. She trusted him; they had common concerns.

"Carmela wants to leave Napoli and take the children," she said. "I told her I would help them."

"Is it possible you could?"

"Yes."

"I pray you will have success. I could support your efforts . . . but not reveal what we discuss tonight." Again, he touched his collar, a gesture of confidentiality. "We have an understanding?"

"We do. I will talk to Carmela tomorrow before I leave. I'll offer her any assistance to make changes in her life and the lives of the children."

"I will do the same. I counsel families after funerals, offer them spiritual guidance, let them know they are not alone. I will encourage her to consider your offer of support."

Antonella looked over Father Vincenzo's shoulder. "Father, Carmela is watching us from a table with friends."

"Does she look upset?"

"Not at all. She's nodding, smiling. Wait . . . she's getting up; she's coming over."

Carmela weaved through the tables to the table, put a hand on Father Vincenzo's shoulder.

"Hello, Father . . . Antonella," she slurred, a bit tipsy. "What a surprise, my priest drinking with my sister-in-law."

"We are having a worthwhile discussion, Carmela. I like your sister-in-law; she's a very intelligent woman."

"She is. Should I pull up a chair and listen?"

Father Vincenzo frowned; Antonella sensed he wanted to keep talking to her and not be interrupted by Carmela.

"Carmela, if could you let us finish what we were talking about," he said. "Trust me please, I'll share it with you later. I may not have time to talk to your sister-in-law, as she leaves tomorrow. We may be able to meet up on my next visit to Milano."

Carmela didn't seem to mind. Father Vincenzo's diplomatic suggestion had smoothed over a potentially awkward situation. Antonella was impressed.

"Oh, of course, Father, please stay here with Antonella," Carmela said. "We'll be together tomorrow anyway. I just wanted to tell you I was pleased you have a chance to get to know each other. By the way, Antonella, have you seen the memorial table?"

"No, I haven't."

She pointed to the semi-private room where they had had dinner two nights ago. "Come over and see it. There are family photos you probably haven't seen before."

They rose from their chairs, leaving wine glasses on the table, and followed Carmela to the room which had been converted from a dining area into a memorial for Salvo. Around the room, floral wreaths, bouquets, and a banner with Salvo's birth and death dates were displayed, along with the opening of Psalm 23, "The Lord is my shepherd, I shall not want."

Among the floral arrangements on the table were pictures of Salvo and the family that Antonella had never seen: his parents holding him in a blanket when he was a baby, when he was in diapers held by his mother on a beach, a teenager on a motorcycle, with Carmela when they were skinny teenagers, their wedding, Easter, and Christmas pictures.

Antonella picked up photos, looking into Salvo's deep, dark eyes and noticed his curly, black hair as a little boy. A gentle boy, even. As a teenager, he was handsome, almost roguish, with a sly grin on his face. Another photo, him laughing while holding a kitten. Still a bit innocent. As Salvo aged, he grew a beard, let his hair grow longer, unkempt, like he wanted to appear wild and reckless. The sly, mischievous grin became an anxious look, revealing uncertainty, restrained emotions. In pictures with his family, he expressed little joy as a father and husband. It must have been painful for Carmela, having so few flattering photos of him with the family.

Neither she nor Marianna were in any photo, possibly because he had discarded them. Salvo had taunted his younger sisters, boasted he was braver, smarter, mocked their girlish voices when their father was not in the room. He taunted them when they were teenagers, saying they were not pretty, would never have boyfriends.

Antonella recalled incidents that she had repressed for years, not wanting to remember the pain. She felt Father Vincenzo's hand on her arm.

"Would you like to take a walk, get some fresh air?"

She didn't want to turn around and face him, fearing he would see her anguish. "No, I'll be OK."

Carmela adjusted the photos, rearranging them so Salvo's younger photos were at the front of the table. "I'm going to get the children; they haven't seen these yet," she said, leaving Antonella and Father Vincenzo alone in the room.

He took her arm, led her back to the table, neither one of them speaking. She didn't want any more Prosecco or salad. She wanted to go back to the hotel and finish packing for tomorrow.

"Thank you," she said as she reached for her purse on the chair and then turned to face him. "I'm going to leave, Father; it's been a long . . . difficult day."

"Yes, it has," he said. "I'll see you at the cemetery tomorrow. I'm glad we had time to talk. In case we can't tomorrow, I wish you the best in our common objective."

She reached into her purse, took out a business card, scribbled her mobile phone number on the back, and handed it to him.

"Please . . . let's stay in touch," she said, her voice trembling. "I want to continue our discussion. Let me know when you'll come to Milano."

CHAPTER THIRTEEN

FRIDAY

Antonella arrived at the police station at 9 a.m. and was escorted to Commissario Belmondo's office, where he waited with a transcriber.

"Please have a seat, *dottoressa*. I know you don't have a lot of time. After we have your statement, we'll have one of our cars escort you to the cemetery."

"Thank you. I have an hour or so. How goes your investigation of the shooting?"

He grimaced, his face tensed like he'd bit his cheek. "Yesterday was a shock," he said, shaking his head in frustration. "The Rocco and Leone clans had arranged a truce of sorts, as I told you. Informants on both sides told us they had agreed on splitting up the area between Soccavo and Pianura. There was dissension in both clans about the truce, but it takes only one dissident to cause problems, like yesterday. A hothead from the Leone clan fired the first two shots but didn't hit anyone. A Rocco member returned the fire and wounded him. Only four were involved in the shooting, including the one you shot. The fourth shooter ran from the scene but we have him on CCTV. We'll find him. The shooting was not planned, just a couple of troublemakers with guns. Both clans even contacted us, promising it won't happen again."

"Do you trust them? After all, they're criminals and murderers."

He shrugged. "They are, but they're also trying to run businesses, even if they are criminals. Both clans have younger radicals who want to take over from older bosses. We hear from informants that the radicals aren't antagonistic toward each other; they want a compromise; kick out the bosses."

"Does that happen—rivals form a coalition?"

"Sometimes. The *sistema* in Napoli is decentralized, not like the Mafia with a strong central boss, *capo di capi*, in Sicilia. Camorra, on the other hand, is dysfunctional, almost an anarchy, run by unstable tyrants and murderers. They're not interested in the common good or helping a rival. It's ruthless greed, as simple as that." He looked at the clock. "Let's get going with your statement. I know you're leaving this afternoon."

For twenty minutes, Antonella recited her testimony about the procession and shooting the man in the doorway. The transcriber worked efficiently and within a minute of Antonella's concluding her statement, she printed a transcript and handed it over to Antonella.

Antonella read through it, picked up a pen from Belmondo's desk, signed it and added her DIGOS rank and identification number. She handed it to Belmondo.

"Before I leave for the cemetery, do you have time for a call with Lucchini?" she asked. "He called me this morning and asked if he could talk to you before I left the station."

"Of course. Do you have his number?"

"Yes," she said, taking out her cell phone and punching in his number.

When Lucchini answered, she greeted him and said, "I just signed a statement about yesterday. I'm in Commissario Belmondo's office. Would you like to talk to him?"

"Please, hand him the phone," he said.

Antonella gave her phone to Belmondo. He put the mobile on speaker, exchanged brief formalities, and then began discussing the shooting during the procession and Antonella wounding the Leone gunman.

"I have Dottoressa Amoruso's statement as well as two from the escort officers who witnessed the shooting," he told Lucchini. "They back up her story. If she hadn't fired, one of our officers could have been hit. She probably saved his life."

"I'm glad she did," Lucchini said. "An officer not on an official assignment still comes to the assistance of a fellow officer in danger. That's why police carry weapons even when they're not on duty. All legal. I'll file a report with the Questura when I get your official statements."

"You'll have them within an hour."

"I've briefed our vice questore," Lucchini said. "He will move it along. But we both know how bureaucracies work—a case like this, an officer from another jurisdiction involved in a shooting, away from their line of duty—the media might get wind of this and try to make it something it isn't. People up the chain of command will want to know all the circumstances before they sign off. Amoruso is highly respected and an experienced officer. I'll make sure it's a routine formality, nothing more than that."

Belmondo smiled. "Giorgio, we've been in the police for a long time. Our bureaucracies are like an octopus with too many tentacles."

Lucchini chuckled. "So true, Pasquale. They can strangle some of our best efforts. We need to feed them information, flattery, protocol, so they don't choke us. I'm sure you're an expert at knowing how to escape their clutches."

"But Giorgio, I'm just a *commissario* in a Napoli suburb," Belmondo said. "You're the capo of a powerful branch of the Interior Ministry in Milano. Many more octopuses there, some giants, I'm sure."

They both laughed. Antonella smiled as she heard both sides of the conversation. Lucchini signed off with, "I hope I see you at a conference soon, Pasquale. We get along well."

"We do, Giorgio. You're lucky to have Dottoressa Amoruso working alongside you. We're deeply indebted to her. I'm glad she was there."

* * * *

The De Cataldo hearse and car with Carmela's family drove under a stone arch of the Santa Maria and Santa Margarita cemetery. Three police cars carried the pallbearers and Carmela's closest friends.

At the entrance, two police cars with officers standing outside blocked incidental traffic until the burial was over. The two-lane paved streets of Pianura shrank to a one-lane asphalt road branching off to different sections of the cemetery.

Ancient palm trees towered over the cemetery rising sporadically from the parched soil. Layers of dried fronds draped from the crowns of the palms like wilted, yellow umbrellas. The ground under the palms was littered with fallen fronds, torn, neglected, and crawling with bugs.

The convoy slowly drove through the cemetery, passing marble monuments and gravestones, many with statues of Mary or Jesus, stone angels, and white crosses. Recent graves were adorned with vases of fresh flowers or wreaths. Older graves languished; a few had chipped vases of bleached plastic flowers, tipped over or smashed.

The procession moved to a far corner of the cemetery along a stone wall defiled with graffiti. Under a palm tree, three men in work clothes of black caps and shirts smoked, watching the small convoy, their shovels on the ground.

A row of metal chairs had been placed by the grave, surrounded by floral wreaths and bouquets. The pallbearers, including Francesco, got out of their car, removed the casket from the hearse, and hoisted it onto their shoulders. They followed Ernesto from De Cataldo's, their feet crunching over dried grass and fallen leaves, resting the casket on metal slats over the grave.

Father Vincenzo, wearing a long white robe, white skull cap, and holding an open Bible stood next to a headstone engraved with Salvo's name and birth date. No death date—it was unknown. Once the casket was in place, Carmela's family and Antonella got out of the car and walked a few steps to the metal chairs.

The pallbearers waited, stepped back, and took their place behind the chairs where Carmela's family sat. They remained standing, Francesco behind Antonella.

Flocks of crows nesting in the palm crowns suddenly burst into the air, squawking and screeching, protesting the intruders below. The mourners looked up at the crows, who flew randomly over the cemetery, diving and swooping, singly and in groups of three and four, like black-feathered missiles. Their squawking intensified as if they were about to launch an aerial assault on the humans below. Then they veered away, soaring above the cemetery, opening their wings and descending to their nests, still screeching.

The noisy racket and audacious aerial display cast an eerie mood over the mourners. Father Vincenzo waited until the disturbance calmed and then raised a hand with two fingers extended. He made a sign of the cross and recited a short prayer.

"Today . . ." he began in a slow, reverent tone, glancing toward the sky, "we consign Salvatore to his final resting place. His soul will join departed loved ones in heaven for eternal rest."

Carmela wept, covering her face with a white handkerchief. Luisa stared at the grave, tears in her eyes, wiped them away with a finger. Diego looked dazed, eyes unfocused, blinking away tears, his hands clutched into fists in his lap. He looked like he was ready to lose control, run, flee from the cemetery and the bad memories. But he didn't. Instead, he sagged onto his mother's shoulder, his face buried in her shawl, weeping. Carmela wrapped an arm around him, leaned over and smoothed a hand over his sobbing face.

Antonella lowered her head and closed her eyes. Father Vincenzo paused, said a short prayer, and ended with "Amen."

Ernesto signaled to the pallbearers; they walked back to their car and got in. Carmela's family stood and walked hand in hand to the gravesite. One by one, Carmela, Luisa, Diego, and Antonella plucked white roses from the bouquets and tossed them onto the casket.

Antonella was the only one not weeping.

* * * * *

Floral arrangements from the funeral had been delivered to Carmela's apartment. When the family arrived at the door later, banners lay on the floor alongside bouquets in vases and wreaths propped up against a wall.

"What are these doing here?" Carmela sputtered, her voice shrill. "Who brought these here? I don't want them! Send them back to the church. I don't need reminders."

"Ugh, they don't look good," Diego said, pointing at a vase of white roses, petals wilted, stems bending over from the heat in the corridor. "Toss them in the garbage."

"No! Wait, Diego," Luisa said, bending over to pick a white rose that hadn't wilted. "I want to keep one to remind me of Papà."

"Oh, gross," Diego said. "He's buried. We just put him in his grave. Why would you want flowers to remember that?"

"Because I do. What's wrong with that?"

"That's stupid. They'll just rot and smell up your room."

"My friend Barbara saved flowers when her *nonna* died. She pressed them in a book to keep forever."

"Why do that?"

"She loved her *nonna*; she wanted memories of her. That was a nice thing to do."

"No, it's not, it's silly."

"Stop it, children," Carmela said, unlocking the door, kicking aside a wreath with the name "Leone" inscribed on it. Diego and Luisa hurried around her and headed down the hallway to their bedrooms.

"Stupid. Picking wilting flowers," Diego said with a snarl before he slammed his door shut.

"Oh God, I'm so sick of this," Carmela muttered as she walked into the kitchen, where pizza boxes and Styrofoam containers with desserts from Vesuvio were stacked on the table. Carmela pushed them to the side and turned to Antonella.

"You want caffè, tea?"

"Tea, please."

"What time is your flight, again? I forgot."

"Four. But I need to drop off the rental car and take the shuttle to the terminal. I should leave no later than two."

Carmela looked at her watch. "Hour and a half. Let's not waste time. Should I fix a little lunch?"

"No, I'm fine."

Carmela filled a pot with water, turned on the stove, and placed the pot over the flames. "Have a seat," she said.

In minutes, they were sipping mint tea. A throb of hip-hop music was reverberating from Diego's room.

"I can't stand that . . . 'music' he listens to. It sounds like jungle drums. It's not really even music; it's just noise."

"A lot of kids like it. I can't listen to it," Antonella said.

Carmela shuddered, closing her eyes. Her face sagged, exhausted with the emotional stresses of the week. "It's over," Carmela said, with a tone of finality. "Finally. I hate what happened, but I can't do anything about it. Salvo's gone. I'm left with two children fighting me every day. I come home from work exhausted, too tired to cook. The kids hide in their rooms. Sometimes I feel like I live alone. And I will be in a few years. I'm a forty-year-old widow, getting older and lonelier by the day, with no hope for the future."

Carmela untied her scarf and tossed it on a chair. It fell to the floor. She didn't pick it up. Antonella let Carmela's cynical declaration hang in the air, waiting to see if she would continue her self-analysis. She did, cursing first.

"*Dannazione*," she huffed, smiled, reached down for her scarf. "Well, I got that off my chest. I've been wanting to curse all morning. I want a glass of wine, but I'll wait until you leave."

"Don't let me stop you."

"No, too early. I don't want the children to think I need a drink to get through the day. What do you think I should do, Antonella? I'm not holding back. I don't want you to, either."

"Being honest with yourself is always the best way."

"Right. That's why I'm dumping everything on you. I'm not going to play a weeping widow. I've been around enough of those, all their playacting, begging for sympathy. They bellow like sheep getting sheared, and everybody gives them attention. For a few hours. But friends forget about it in a day or so. Weeping widows rarely recover. I see them at mass saying rosaries for their dead husbands. Then they show up at Vesuvio and drink wine with other widows. Some nights we have two or three tables with these widows, always sitting in the same chairs like they're schoolchildren. They're pitiful. Men stay away from them. They're like snared rabbits. They can't escape because they play the victims of the *sistema*. Nobody likes to be around victims. And I won't do that. I'm not a victim! I'm a widow . . . with many years ahead of me. I want to live them, not merely endure."

Carmela was purging a flood of anger, frustration, and fear. This was a side she had been revealing since the night at Vesuvio, when she started talking more openly than she ever had before. Now she was begging for help. Antonella wasn't going to let it pass by. It was a rare moment that might not come again.

"Carmela, I want to help. I've not been in your situation, so I speak only from seeing friends who've experienced the death of a family member.

You're not alone. I hear your anger and sense of despair. It's important you make decisions so your life has meaning and purpose again."

"Yes! How? Tell me!"

"If you had fantasies or expectations that things might work out without making changes, you're deceiving yourself. Life is hard—"

"Hard! Worse than that. Life can be hell! Believe me, I know."

Antonella waited to see if she was going to say more. They stared at each other; Carmela's eyes flared like she had seen a ghost. She reached across and grabbed Antonella's hand.

"I'm sorry, I'm sorry," she apologized. "I'm not going crazy, I'm really not. It's just that now that Salvo is buried, I have to move on. I want to move on. The last couple of years my life has been a hurricane, a tornado, whatever it is in the ocean."

"Tsunami?" Antonella said, appreciating how Carmela was releasing her emotions with little regard for decorum.

"Yes, tsunami! My life has been a tsunami. I don't want a tsunami. Life goes on," Carmela babbled, her voice breaking, her eyes blinking rapidly. "People I know, friends, will get up tomorrow morning and resume their lives. But I can't . . . it's not going to be easy."

"It never is," Antonella nodded. "What are your options?"

"Not good if I stay here. I'll rot. The children will drive me crazy; they know that I'm not managing well. They see it. And one day, they'll leave home. Diego will get in trouble . . . more heartache," she shuddered. "Luisa has a boyfriend I don't like. He's a creep, touching her where he shouldn't. He curses and knows it makes me mad. My blood boils when I see him with her."

"Does she love him?"

She shook her head. "No. I don't think so, anyway. He flirts, tells her silly things like he can't live without her and wants to marry her. That's a joke. Of course, he says things like that, but all he wants to do is—" she stopped and shook her head. "But I sense she's getting over him. He says sarcastic things about her violin, says she's wasting her time and should become a model. He said with her body, she should be modeling bikinis or lingerie—disgusting! A couple of weeks ago, I caught him trying to sneak into her room when she was changing clothes! I kicked him out of the apartment, told him never to come back. And he hasn't, that creep!"

Antonella was shocked, imagining how a boy preying on her daughter would be terrifying for Carmela. She had no idea how to respond.

Carmela reached into her purse and took out her cigarettes, lighting one and sucking in a deep drag. When she exhaled, she coughed and continued. "Glad I got that off my chest. Sorry to share such terrible things. It's not your concern, of course, but it's part of the reason I'm so angry. I'm relieved that Luisa loves her music and doesn't care about fashion or modeling."

"She's talented, Carmela," Antonella said. "I don't think her passion is something she will give up."

"I hope she'll continue to practice. I don't know what that would lead to, but anything is better than ending up as a waitress in a pizzeria like me. I'm not a waitress anymore, but that's the only job I could find after I had the kids. At least I'm a shift manager, but that's the end of the line if I stay here. But I don't want to be just a pizzeria manager; no, I don't."

She took a long drag on her cigarette, exhaled, and, shaking her head, looked at Antonella.

"Are you ready to leave Napoli?" Antonella asked.

"Yes!"

"You've lived here your whole life—how can you leave?"

"I have to, I don't want any of it anymore," she said, sweeping her arms around the kitchen as if rejecting it all. "There's too much here that will drag me down. Same for the children. I can't escape the past, but I don't want it to be the future. Take it all . . . throw it out the window," she said, gesturing to the window.

"When?"

"Soon. I don't want to wait."

Antonella rose from her chair, walked around the table, letting the finality in Carmela's response linger. Would Carmela back off from her declarations to leave? Antonella waited to see if Carmela had anything else to say.

Carmela looked up at Antonella, standing across the table from her. When she spoke, her voice was calm, as if she were asking someone to pass the salt and pepper.

"What should I do? Tell me, Antonella."

Antonella paused. "What about Diego? Can he leave Napoli and not be angry with you?"

Carmela looked at her. Antonella sensed she was ready to confess something. But she got up instead.

"Let's ask him." She crushed her cigarette in an ashtray, went through the kitchen into the hallway, and rapped on both bedroom doors.

"Ragazzi, come out. Zia Antonella is leaving soon. She wants to talk to you."

They came out, sat down at the kitchen table, drained of energy, listless.

"Mamma, I want to go back to my room. I'm tired and upset," Diego said.

"We all are. Antonella has a question for you."

Antonella hesitated, thinking of how she could ask Diego without turning him off.

"First of all, I want to thank you and your sister for letting me see how you're growing up. Soon, in a couple of years, you will be adults and have to make important decisions."

"I'm ready," Diego said confidently. "But Mamma won't let me. She thinks I'm still her *bambino*."

"No I don't, Diego," Carmela said. "Just listen to your *zia*."

"What do you want to do the next couple years, Diego?"

"I don't know . . . maybe leave school," he said with a shrug. "Get a job, make some money so I can buy a motorcycle."

"That's a joke!" Luisa protested. "You couldn't get a job. Who would hire you? You're lazy; you hate to work. You can't keep your room clean. When Mamma's not home, you don't even help me heat up dinner. Or clean the table. You just hide in your room, listen to weird music, or play video games."

"And what do you do?" he asked. "Talk on the phone all day, text your friends, smoke cigarettes, hang out with your sleazy boyfriend who grabs your ass—"

"Stop it!" Carmela said. "Quit arguing; I'm sick of it. Antonella has to go home—and you just argue. Grow up."

Diego scowled at Luisa and then at his mother. Luisa looked away and folded her arms over her chest, her lips pressed together.

"I won't be able to come back to Napoli this summer," Antonella said. "Expo will take up all my time. Millions of people from all over the world will come. The people in my office won't have vacations until it's over at the end of October."

"Can we go to Expo, Mamma?" Diego asked.

"Ask your *zia*."

"Can we, Zia Antonella?"

"Yes, I can get tickets, and you can stay in our apartment."

"Really?" Luisa said, snapping her head around. "I love your apartment."

"We have a spare bedroom. I can rearrange my office into another guest room."

"Mamma, let's go!" Luisa exclaimed.

"Yeah, it'll be fun," Diego agreed. "I want to go to a soccer game, see AC Milan at San Siro stadium. I watch them on TV."

"My husband can get tickets for you, Diego. Luisa, a friend teaches violin and cello. You could have lessons."

"Oh, please, I want to!"

"Diego, my husband Carlo knows people who manage restaurants. They train chefs and waiters to work in their restaurant. Maybe you could go to a couple classes, learn more about making pizzas. You're too young to have a job officially, but you could learn."

"Yes! Could I learn how fancy restaurants make pizza, not just the way we do it at Vesuvio?"

"I think you could."

"I want to make pasta, too. Roll the dough like we do for pizzas, but then you put it into a cool machine that makes fettuccine, pappardelle, spaghetti, and other kinds. I want to learn how they do that. And learn about sauces, too. And cooking fish, I want to know how you do all that."

Antonella looked at Carmela watching her children, enjoying their excitement and imagining going to Milano instead of remaining in Napoli, bickering with each other. She glanced back at Antonella, made an almost imperceptible nod.

"OK, ragazzi, we'll do it. We'll take a vacation when school is out," Carmela said. "Milano is a very exciting city with a lot of history. We'll go to the lakes, too, and ride ferries. The mountains are amazing, and all the lakes have beautiful gardens."

"Mamma, would you really take us, maybe spend the summer there? It's so hot in Napoli; I can't stand it. It would be fun to go swimming in the lakes," Luisa said, looking hopefully at her mother and aunt.

"Yes, I will," Carmela nodded, smiling at the children. "Zia Antonella said she would help plan our summer."

"Wow, that would be super!" Diego said. "I want to learn how to paddle boats or kayaks, maybe even water ski, to take jet ski lessons, even. I've seen it on TV."

"Luisa said with a giggle, "Oooo, that would be so much fun! When can we come, Zia Antonella?"

CHAPTER FOURTEEN

SATURDAY

Antonella woke at 5:30 a.m., an hour earlier than most Saturday mornings. Her sleep had been restless, just as it had been the previous Saturday, when she'd gone to the funeral of her friend, Cristina. Six days. Two funerals.

A wave of depression swept over her before she even opened her eyes. How could fate plunge you into a macabre scenario of attending two funerals in less than a week? Cristina and Salvo—two people gone forever from her life.

Antonella disliked funerals, and even more so when Carlo was not with her. His attitude toward funerals was more thoughtful and deliberative, saying that funerals gave families and friends an opportunity to reminisce and say gracious things about the departed.

"Sharing memories is important for mourners," he had counseled. "You might meet someone you haven't seen in a long time. Plus, you have the opportunity to share a story about the departed, usually a cherished memory or a humorous event. Funerals don't have to dwell on grief—it's also a time for reflection."

OK, Carlo. But I found few people who had much good to say about Salvo. Francesco was one; Father Vincenzo, the other. Being with Carmela and the children was the only good thing about the week. That was the legacy of Salvo's funeral.

She opened her eyes, arose, walked into the bathroom. The mirror was not her friend today. Puffy bags under her eyes, sagging cheeks, and a tangle of hair clumped on one side where she had slept all night. Her mouth felt like sand. She drank a glass of water to slake her thirst. And a second. Her mirror told her story: eight hours of sleep, but little rest.

Caffè . . . she needed caffè. She walked into the kitchen and ground coffee for her Moka. While she waited for the water to boil, she thought of Carlo coming home Tuesday. They would talk a few hours from now, evening in Sydney, morning in Milano. Wait . . . was he still in Sydney? Didn't he mention going to Adelaide or Melbourne over the weekend? Whatever he had told her, she had forgotten.

The caffè was refreshing. In a few seconds, the caffeine injection awakened her brain. Moment by moment, her morning anxiety receded, sleeping muscles awoke, eyes focused, a pink glow on her cheeks.

The shrill siren of a passing ambulance on the street below energized her. She was ready for the day. She began making mental notes of what she had to do today: Minor duties around the apartment. Finish unpacking. Do some laundry. Jot down a list of food to buy at the market. Retrieve the week's mail. Go to the office. Yes, Saturday at the office for a few hours. She couldn't wait.

Returning to the Questura would be like another jolt of caffeine. The office was where she felt motivated, eager to talk to colleagues who showed up Saturday mornings for a couple of hours. Catch up on classified reports from the week. Check next week's calendar. Respond to a long list of emails unopened since Monday afternoon. Giorgio had texted the previous evening that he would be in the office around 2 p.m. They could discuss her week in Napoli.

As she showered and dressed casually, she knew she was forgetting something. What was it? The thought had come to her when she was flying from Capodichino to Linate. Not a domestic errand. Not related to the office. Not about Carlo. Something she was supposed to do today . . . what was it? She couldn't remember. When she grabbed her purse and was ready to leave the apartment, she remembered.

She dropped her purse and went to her desk. The idea was to write a letter to Carmela. Not a phone call or a text. A letter, like the kind she and Rosanna had talked about at dinner Wednesday night. Writing a letter was like being with a person face to face. A personal letter with carefully crafted sentences, expressing emotion, compassion, and connection.

She grabbed a sheet of copy paper and a pen. She wouldn't write the letter now, just sketch out a few thoughts. The blank sheet of paper stared up at her. Her pen was poised but not writing. She wasn't sure how to begin. Then she began scribbling a greeting, thanks for inviting her to their home . . . their brief time together . . . Diego and Luisa . . . Vesuvio . . . the funeral, burial, and talking at her apartment yesterday before she left. The invitation to come to Milano.

She glanced up at the clock. Twenty-four hours ago, she was at the burial, a somber ritual punctuated by the soaring, screeching crows just as Father Vincenzo began his prayer. Antonella had glanced at the children. Diego's mouth was open as he stared at the noisy crows, a terrified look on his face. Luisa had shut her eyes and put her hands over her ears. Would that disturbing incident haunt them when they remembered their father's burial?

Antonella scratched out notes about the funeral and the cemetery. Carmela didn't need to be reminded of either. More about the future, coming to Milano as she hoped. Expressions of the family healing.

By the time she finished an outline, it was three pages long. She'd buy nice stationery that afternoon. She read through the draft, moderately pleased how it read but still wanting time to think more about it before she composed it.

She'd wait until tonight when she was home alone. After the office and talking with Giorgio. And Carlo. She needed a full twenty-four hours in Milano before she'd turn the outline into a composed letter. She wanted time to reflect on the comfort and security of being home, distanced from enduring five days of the family grieving in Napoli.

* * * * *

Antonella sipped from a water bottle, her feet propped on a bottom desk drawer, reading glasses perched on her nose, leisurely scrolling through the email messages that had come in the previous week.

She felt revived now that she was at DIGOS reading classified police reports and commenting with suggestions based upon her years of experience. She felt alert, in control, far from Napoli. Away from conflicts, disturbing incidents, and people trapped by life's circumstances. But the memories of Salvo's funeral—the procession, the shooting, the wake at Vesuvio, the cemetery—still lingered in her mind.

She was reading a detailed report on Expo security when she heard Lucchini's familiar voice.

"Welcome back, Antonella; it's good to see you at your desk again."

"Giorgio!" She said, getting up from her desk to greet him. "It's *so* good to be home. Whoever thought the office would be a sanctuary? I couldn't wait to get here this morning."

"You're energized! I thought you'd be exhausted from the week."

"Oh, I am, but also grateful. The best part of traveling is coming home."

"It is." He sat down in front of her desk and set his briefcase on an empty chair. "And your life will be back to normal when Carlo comes home."

"Tuesday night. I really miss him. We talked a couple times, but the time differences between Napoli and Australia are challenging."

"Tell me about your week; I know there was a lot you couldn't get into with texts or brief calls."

She took off her reading glasses, leaned back in her chair. "Let me start with Tuesday morning," she started. "I met Luisa at the apartment; she was practicing for a violin lesson that afternoon and played for me. She's got talent, enough to get her out of Napoli and away from the criminal environment. I met Diego and Carmela that night after seeing Commissario Belmondo at the station. Carmela feels trapped. She works in a pizzeria owned by the Rocco *sistema*. I'm sure they supplement her salary because of Salvo's death and paid to fix up their apartment and buy Luisa's violin. Who knows what else?"

"You said the violin was from Cremona?"

"Can you believe that? It must have cost a couple thousand euros."

"Camorra clans look after families, paying them off so they don't go *pentiti* and confess to the police," Lucchini said. "But money doesn't heal the emotional wounds when a family member is arrested or murdered."

"I witnessed that, certainly. Carmela opened up to me at the pizzeria in a way she never had when Salvo was alive. I hoped things would improve between us, and they did. I didn't see the family again until Thursday at the funeral, and of course, you know about the shooting. After that unfortunate incident, I took them to my hotel, where they'd be safe. Again, Carmela confided in me, expressed how unhappy she was and how she didn't want to stay in Napoli. After the cemetery yesterday, we went back to their apartment and had another talk. She was desperate, almost begging for help. So, I invited them to come to Milano this summer for Expo and a holiday, which they certainly need after the last two years."

"Really?"

Antonella nodded. "She and Luisa can stay in our guest bedroom, and I'll rearrange my home office for Diego. If things go well, Carmela said they'd consider staying in the area and getting an apartment in the suburbs so the kids can enroll in good schools."

"You and Carlo would do that?"

"Why not? We don't have children, only two nieces in Bologna. Diego and Luisa are our extended family."

"You're offering them a lifeline, starting over in a safer location. That's a challenge for you and Carlo."

"It is. Carmela and I talked it over in general but not in detail. Carlo is a generous person who's helped friends before and contributes to charities. He has a good heart. Fortunately, we're able to help them at a critical time."

"What type of commitment do you see? Months, years?"

"Not years, a few weeks, a couple months, maybe. By then Carmela could be situated so she could get a job and get the kids back in school."

Giorgio frowned. "Finding a job is never easy, especially around Milano."

"But she's worked in restaurants, as a manager even. I think she could find something suitable to get back on her feet. Time will tell if Carmela takes me up on it. I'm a little anxious about it, to be honest. Playing hostess to relatives for a couple weeks in the summer is one thing. Taking responsibility for the future lives of three people is an obligation. I just wish it wasn't this summer."

"You won't have much free time with Expo going on."

"She knows. But Carlo's summer travel schedule is limited. He has friends who have Airbnb apartments in the summer for tourists. They usually stay only a week or two, so he'd ask them to hold open times for them. One friend said he'd give them a discount since they're family."

"Do you really think they'd leave Napoli and relocate here?"

"Too early to say. But Carmela wants to go back to school, finish her degree, and get a professional job."

"What will she do for money?"

"According to her, she has money saved and will get more when a new partner takes over Sal's interest in the motorcycle shop. She'll need that, since she'll have sole responsibility for raising two independent teenagers. Well, she's already had that responsibility since Salvo disappeared. But it's not just finances; Carmela needs emotional strength to start a new life in a new place far from Napoli."

"That's a lot to expect of a recent widow raising two teenagers."

"It is, but I heard her determination to take on the challenge. No idea if she'll marry again; she's not in a good emotional state to do more than just take care of herself and the children. That would be a disaster for any man. I doubt it will happen, at least for a couple of years . . . I hope. Time will tell."

"What about her extended family in Campania? Do you think Carmela is strong enough to leave? Or would she just give up and stay in Napoli?"

"Her parents died when she was in her twenties. She has a couple of cousins and a much older brother who lives in Palermo. They're not that close; he canceled plans to come to the funeral at the last minute. That made her mad, but I sensed she wasn't really looking forward to seeing him. She let me know she and the children consider me family, even though we hadn't been close before."

"You bonded well over just a few days."

"We did. I'm going to write a letter to her tonight agreeing to their visit, but with conditions. I sketched a draft this morning. I want to make clear that they're welcome but must comply with our requests. I'm concerned about Diego's attitude and hope that we can get him interested in learning about cooking and eventually working in a restaurant when he's old enough. Luisa will adapt easier once she starts violin lessons and goes to concerts. I'll get tickets to La Scala and take the whole family. It could be a great experience for them."

They looked at each other without speaking; Antonella tapped a pen on her thigh, her jaw firm like when she contemplated a challenging issue. Giorgio looked into his paper coffee cup. Moments of shared silence were not unusual for them. They didn't fill the air with banal pleasantries or empty thoughts.

Giorgio said finally, "You were gone a week; look what happened."

"Five days," she corrected. "Monday night until last night."

"Monday, you were dreading going. You return Friday motivated and with a plan. I'm impressed."

"Things can change fast during a family crisis, Giorgio," she said as she waved a hand, brushing aside the compliment. "Carmela was grieving, depressed, barely able to manage the kids. But she expressed determination to make serious, life-changing decisions to start over.

"I went for the funeral and witnessed a distressed family, not unexpected under the circumstances. But the immediacy of the crisis is powerful when you are there, witnessing the grief and pain. That doesn't come through in a phone call or an email. The intensity of witnessing makes you—or at least me—want to help relieve the pain.

"Watching Luisa play her violin was an inspiration. A daughter grieving for her father but lost in music. Diego was rude when I met him Tuesday night, until he started talking about becoming a chef. I saw those incidents as hopeful. But Carmela is the key. When she repeated that she wanted to make changes in her life and sought my advice, that was the signal to help them."

"You were the catalyst."

She nodded. "I suppose you could say that."

"You're proposing a serious commitment to them."

"They're my family now."

"Let me know if I can help," Lucchini said as he stood to leave.

She smiled. "Oh wait, Giorgio, sit down; I have something else to tell you. Two things actually."

"What's that?"

Her smile brightened, and she chuckled. "I was almost assaulted on the street Tuesday night."

"Whoa, what happened?"

"A couple boys, street thugs, tried to snatch my purse and push me into the street."

"No! Really?"

"I snapped back the fingers of one boy trying to get my purse and jammed my heel into the foot of another behind me. Crushed a couple of toes, I think." She smiled.

"Good for you," Giorgio laughed. "They didn't know who they were dealing with."

"Then, Salvo's business partner, Francesco, whom I hadn't met, kicked the boys, grabbed my arm, and pulled me away. I saw him the next day at the motorcycle shop, and he told me things about Salvo I didn't know. Pretty sad, actually."

"I'm sorry. Was there something else?"

She nodded and then grinned again. "I found out the Rocco clan had paid for Salvo's casket. I went there, told them I wouldn't allow it, and insisted I pay for the casket."

"Really, how did that go? You were interfering with a Camorra tradition, I'm sure."

"I could care less," she said, shaking her head. "Funerals should be financed by the family if they can afford it, not criminal thugs whose actions led to the murder."

Lucchini frowned. "I'm sure they found out about it. Did you hear anything?"

She shook her head. "Nah, just a few phone calls behind a curtain when I told the head of the mortuary I was going to pay. I couldn't hear what was said, but after a few minutes, she came back and said she accepted it."

"Good for you," he said, smiling. "A lot more happened in Napoli than attending a funeral and helping a family."

"Yes, a few *camorristi* learned they don't always get the last word," she boasted.

* * * * *

Carmela —

I write this letter with love for you and your family. I also write it with concern about your future and with the hope that you will have the courage to make major changes in your lives. Luisa and Diego need your strength.

We had brief but meaningful conversations about this and other issues. I stand by everything I told you—an offer to come to Milano and to stay at our apartment. You will have an opportunity to go on holiday with the children, which I know you haven't managed to do in years.

Consider our home yours for the summer. We'll set rules, but they will mostly be about expected behavior and respect for our property and time. No need to pay for meals or food; we'll be happy to take care of that. Carlo and I have very demanding schedules and won't be available all the time. We trust you will take responsibility for ensuring Luisa and Diego respect our conditions.

Tell me the dates you would like to stay here. Two or three weeks seems best, plus another week or two if you take a holiday to the lakes. We can help with travel arrangements and suggestions when you are here.

You must respect my work responsibilities. I will be in the office most days, including weekends, until late. A maid cleans and cooks twice a week for us. I will ask her to come every day if you would like. I know you will treat her with respect and kindness. You and the children need to take care of cleaning your rooms and helping with laundry. Lunches and dinners can be prepared by my maid, but you are welcome to help her. Make this clear with her, don't change your mind, and be sure to fulfill your promises.

When you arrive, you and I will have a long talk about your plans, expectations, and schedule for the summer. Be decisive. Think things through before you leave Napoli. Come with an agenda and a calendar.

Please think seriously about this. Share with me your questions or concerns. I don't work well with people who are not honest, direct, and committed. You are faced with a situation that requires you to be decisive and positive. If you can't be either, this summer will not work out. Tell me what you expect and are committed to before you leave.

Please respond to this letter in a week. With another letter, not a phone call, email, or text. Take your time, think through what I'm writing, and share what you hope and fear.

Carlo and I will cooperate to help you and your family. We will have serious talks with you and offer suggestions and ideas that might help you.

Be open to what we have to offer. Tell us your limitations. We need total honesty.

Carmela, our past relationship was superficial. I still don't know you as well as I wish I did. You confided in me last week, and I began to see a person I want to know better. I hope we continue to share confidences and grow closer.

I don't dwell on the past. We can't change anything that happened a minute, an hour, a day, or a month ago. It's the past. I deal only with decisions about making a better and safer present and future.

Let's plan for a better and safer future—yours, Luisa's, and Diego's.
Carlo and I await your visit.
With love,
Antonella

THE END

BIBLIOGRAPHY

Dickie, John. *Blood Brotherhoods: A History of Italy's Three Mafias*. New York: Public Affairs, 2014.

Ferrante, Elena. *My Brilliant Friend*. Translated by Ann Goldstein. New York: Europa Editions, 2012.

Ginsborg, Paul. *Italy and Its Discontents: Family, Civil Society, State, 1980–2001*. Penguin; New Ed edition, 2001.

Ortese, Anna Maria. *Neapolitan Chronicles*. Translated by Ann Goldstein and Jenny McPhee, 2018. New York: New Vessel Press, 1994. Previously published as *Il Mare Non Bagna Napoli* (1953).

Reski, Petra. *The Honored Society: A Portrait of Italy's Most Powerful Mafia*. Translated by Shaun Whiteside. New York: Nation Books, 2008.

Saviano, Roberto. *Gomorrah*. Translated by Virginia Jewiss. New York: Picador, 2007. Previously published as *Gomorra* (2006).

Saviano, Roberto. *The Piranhas: The Boy Bosses of Naples*. Translated by Anthony Shugaar. New York: Farrar, Straus & Giroux, 2018. Previously published as *La Paranza dei Bambini* (2016).

Taylor, Benjamin. *Naples Declared: A Walk Around the Bay*. New York: Penguin, 2012.

ACKNOWLEDGMENTS

Writing a novel is a journey best undertaken with the support and encouragement of many people. Friends and associates in Italy and the US were with me while I was researching and writing *Vesuvius Nights*. Elena Ciampella, Benedetta Calzavara, Eric Sylvers, Caterina Cutrupi, Bojana Murisic, Marco Ottaviano, and high-level sources in Milano's Questura helped me with important details for the plot and characters. Tina Carignani was my researcher and talented guide in Napoli, who revealed to me parts of her beloved hometown that most casual visitors would never experience. Tina also interpreted during meetings with police sources at the Napoli Questura.

Pamela McManus, Wendy Sizer, Doug Kennedy, Alessandra Rosetti, Danica Alvarado, and Nick Bermudez continue to be resources and close friends. Heather Pendley, my editor, helped me with final drafts, and in my opinion, produced an excellent book. Thanks, and welcome to Tina and Heather, two new members of my writing team.

ABOUT THE AUTHOR

Jack Erickson writes in multiple genres: international thrillers, mysteries, true crime, short mysteries, and romantic suspense. He is currently writing the *Milan Thriller* series featuring the anti-terrorism police, DIGOS, at Milan's Questura (police headquarters). Book 1 in the series is *Thirteen Days in Milan*. Book 2, *No One Sleeps,* was published in 2017. Book 4 in the series, *The Lonely Assassin,* will be published in 2020.

The models for Erickson's thrillers are three popular Italian mystery series: Donna Leon's Commissario Brunetti (Venice), Andrea Camilleri's Inspector Salvo Montalbano (Sicily), and Michael Dibdin's Commissario Aurelio Zen (Rome). All three have been produced as TV series on networks such as BBC, PBS, RAI, or Deutsche Welle.

Erickson travels throughout Italy to research and sample Italian contemporary life and culture. Earlier in life, he was an Air Force officer, a U.S. Senate speechwriter, a Washington-based editor, and publisher for RedBrick Press. He wrote and published several books on the emerging craft-brewing industry, including the award-winning *Star Spangled*

Beer: A Guide to America's New Microbreweries and Brewpubs. He lives in Northern California with his wife.

We hope you enjoyed reading *Vesuvius Nights* and will write a review on your favorite digital site. Reviews are important for authors but also for readers looking for their next book.

Sign up for Erickson's email newsletter at:

www.jackerickson.com

www.RedBrickPress.net

The Milan Thriller Series

Thirteen Days in Milan

Sylvia de Matteo, an American single mother, is taken hostage by terrorists during a political assassination at *Stazione Centrale,* Milan's train station.

Sylvia is seized at gunpoint, thrown into the back of a van, blindfolded, beaten, and driven to a warehouse where she is imprisoned in a cell.

Moments after she is captured, a Paris-bound train with Sylvia's fiancé and ten-year-old daughter aboard departs *Centrale* without Sylvia.

When the terrorists discover that Sylvia's father is a wealthy Wall Street investment banker, they demand a ransom for her safe release.

No One Sleeps

Milan's elite anti-terrorism DIGOS police receive a tip that a sleeper cell of Muslim terrorists has received toxic chemicals from Pakistan to make deadly sarin gas.

The terrorist leader has access to Milan's centers of finance, technology, commerce, and entertainment—all high-profile targets with hundreds of casualties in the event of a terrorist attack.

Vesuvius Nights

Antonella Amoruso, senior deputy of Milan's anti-terrorism police, receives a call to return to her hometown of Naples for the funeral of a family member murdered in a Camorra clan feud.

Amoruso is plunged into the dangerous culture of the Camorra, Naples's violent crime syndicate, which thrives on illegal drugs, prostitution, extortion, and murder. Her goal is to rescue her family from the Camorra's deadly grip.

The Lonely Assassin

Dmitri Volkov embezzles millions by laundering money in Switzerland for Russian oligarchs. He flees with his Italian wife to a remote location near Milan, where their daughter lives.

Putin wants him dead. He sends a GRU assassin to Milan to find and poison Volkov.

The assassin travels to Milan with phony documents and a vial of toxic poison. Unexpectedly, he meets an intriguing Italian woman who probes into his emotional life. On a dangerous assignment, he realizes he's an assassin in deep personal crisis.

Made in the USA
Middletown, DE
27 August 2020